DANCING DRAGON MAGIC

DIALOGUES IN CLAY

Susan Smith James

Happy Publishing

Living in Magic!

One night, I dreamt that I had a shape shifting hat. I don't know if the hat shape shifted or if wearing the hat gave you the ability to shape shift, but I was happy to wear it!

The hat was made of purple velvet, with a profusion of flowers that seemed to also be made of various colors of velvet. It was sort of like a top hat in shape, but it was soft, and instead of standing up tall like a top hat, the velvet flowers came out of the top and spilled down one side, making the whole thing slump over. The velvet brim was a bit more stiff, but still softer than a real top hat.

I took a course in duality, and the first part of the course dealt with grounding. All that grounding made me feel short, like my feet were mired in six inches of mud. I did not have (or at least not remembered) any fanciful dreams since. One night, I woke up at around 3AM. I announced to the room that I was tired of all this being stuck to the ground and I wanted to fly, to be magic, to wear my shape shifting hat!

The Night Dragon came to me and told me to stop grounding myself to the center of the planet, to instead send a connection up to the ionosphere. Then I would be able to fly between the earth and the sky, like the Shuman Resonance does. He said that my body is part of the earth, and it cannot be anything else. My spirit may leave the ionosphere, but not without effort, and in any case, Gaia knows and loves me, just as any other part of herself. She will not let anything happen while I'm inside her aura.

And with that, Gaia herself, gave me a jacket of iridescent purple velvet, to go with my hat and to protect me as I "live in magic."

I am not sure how to proceed to "live in magic", but I am happy with my hat and coat, and feel that I am ready to experience whatever it is.

THE NIGHT DRAGON

It was black, dark and inky as night could get. Using his last few moments before the dawn struck and killed his fun, The Night Dragon sensed the coming of the light. Was it through sight, or smell, or a shiver of his scales, no matter? Should he hide within a cave and wait until the light burned itself out, or fly to the west, following his element? 'Am I getting old?' he thought. There was a time when he would not hesitate to circle the planet endlessly, always remaining with the darkness. "Bah," he chuckled, his voice deep and resonate. "Time is a lie. I have no less time than when I began, and that was before the dark and the light separated." He turned to the west and silently flew into the darkness.

THE SUN DRAGON

Heat radiates from him, his scales glowing, like molten glass in a furnace. He prefers to fly, always hovering above the ground. In fact, he can't land without protective spells, lest he set the ground on fire. He thinks of it like slippers on his feet, but he must be vigilant of his tail, one touch can ignite anything. So, he mostly sticks to the sky, landing occasionally on the tops of volcanoes, to take soothing mineral baths in the lava.

It was during one of these baths that he saw The Night Dragon, flying past. "Greetings my brother," he cried. "How goes it with you?" "As always," said The Night Dragon as he circled the volcano. "Yes, isn't it glorious?" replied The Sun Dragon. "As perfect as it has ever been, brother," said The Night Dragon. They both broke into peals of laughter, the sky filling with smoke and cloud, from their breath.

THE MOON DRAGON

She never flies, she simply levitates and hovers. She glides silently, with only a shimmer of light to announce her presence. She prefers it cool and quiet. She mostly keeps to herself, but looks down vigilantly from her high place. What is she looking for? Peace. It is her self-appointed job to observe peace and encourage it to grow, wherever she finds it. When she encounters discord, or strife, she hovers over that place and meditates on spreading peace. Like a soothing ointment, it can calm the inflamed, cool the fire and quiet the disruption, almost without notice. Few wield more power than she.

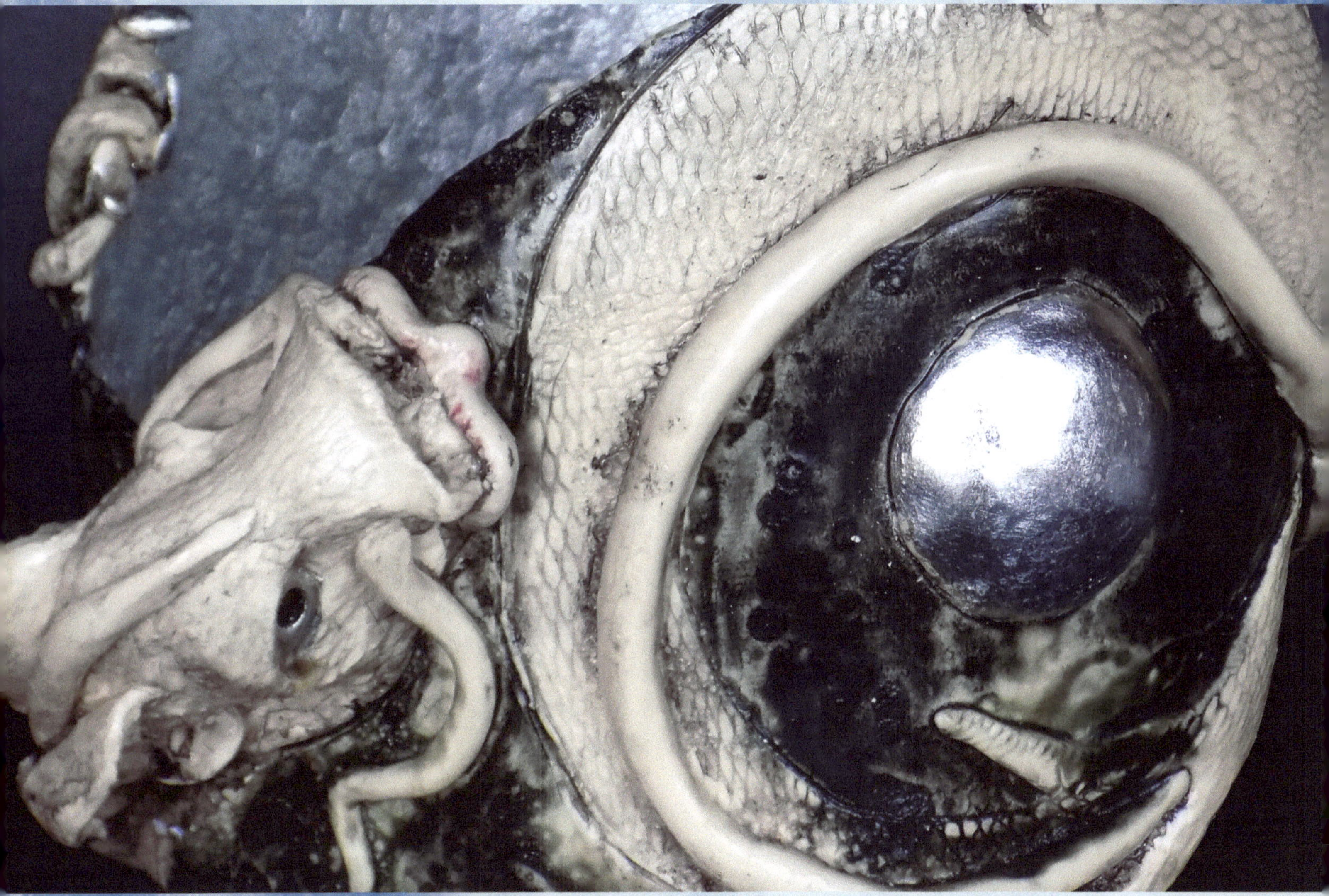

THE DRAGON OF THE DAY

Like a rainbow arched over the sky, The Day Dragon revels in beauty and color. She is constantly dancing, playing and singing her triumphant song of joy. She is creating wind with her wings, clouds with her breath and spreading warmth with her body. She is a favorite playmate of The Sun Dragon. They can often be found dancing together through the sky.

"Hello fair Day, how well do I find you?" asked The Sun Dragon. "Well indeed, hot one," replied Day. "The sky is fine for a dance." "Indeed, it is," answered Sun. "Who shall keep the rhythm?" "Why I shall sing as we dance," said Day. And dance they did, all the way across the wide sky.

THE SEA DRAGON

She is one of the largest dragons you will ever find. Sea is slippery and sleek, fast both above and below the waterline. Like a behemoth ship, she can use her wings like giant sails, to skim her shimmering body over the swelling waves. Under the water, she flies as well as any dragon of the air, diving, twisting, and undulating through her salty domain.

She often speaks to her friend The Moon Dragon, when the waters are calm and peaceful, because of Moon's presence. "Hello fair dragon, how goes it this night?" inquired Sea. "Tranquil and soft as far as I can see, my large, sleek friend," replied Moon. "And what of your mission of peace this night?" asked Sea. "You can judge for yourself, are the waters turbulent tonight?" responded Moon. "The waters are like a deep black mirror," answered Sea. "I know you prefer a bit more action than this!" said Moon. "I shall stir up the surface with a great leap and dive, when you have crossed the horizon, dear one, for now, I am content," said Sea. "As we all should be" spoke Moon.

THE RIVER DRAGON

Much smaller than his aunt, Sea, River is a long water dragon. Because his preferred home is in rivers, both big and small, he has an amazing ability to change size. He can be like a small serpent or a large ship. His color shifts from clear and green to muddy brown. He is very difficult to spot when he is submerged. Like all dragons, he can sit and meditate like a rock, or move as swiftly as thought itself.

THE RAIN DRAGON

Being a water dragon of the air is no easy thing. He must always follow the clouds or risk drying out. Sometimes he finds refuge in a rain forest, where his scales stay nice and moist. Storms are his favorite playgrounds, as he can play with his friends, Lightning and Thunder there. They play tag, and hide and seek. Sometimes their fun lasts for days.

A CONVERSATION BETWEEN THE SUN DRAGON AND THE RIVER DRAGON

The Sun Dragon spotted The River Dragon lying belly up in a small river. He circled in his flight, wondering if something was wrong with the youngster. "Hail young River, how are you this fine day" shouted Sun, rather louder than he had intended. The River Dragons eyes shot open, and he jumped to his feet in the shallow water. "Oh, hello Sir Sun" replied River, breathlessly, "You startled me!" The Sun Dragon landed tentatively on some nearby rocks along the bank, there was a slight hiss as steam rose from the wet rocks. "I thought you might be ill, laying belly up like that" said Sun. "I was just warming up my underside, Sir, I guess I fell asleep" replied River. "Well that's fine then" said Sun "How are your studies coming along?" "Fine Sir, I've been contemplating the light" said River. "Is there anything I could help you with, I have been around a very long time, perhaps you have questions I can answer?" said Sun, moving to sit on a large rock. "Well, thank you, Sir, I do wonder about some things" responded River. He thought for a while, The Sun Dragon sat patiently.

"I have been observing the light, sunlight, moonlight, reflected light, things that have their own light and things that mirror the light of others," stated The River Dragon. "Is all light good and all dark evil?" River asked. "Hold on there, Young River," said Sun. "Why do you think light is good and dark is evil?" "Isn't it, Sir?" asked River. "Not at all," replied Sun. "Light and dark are necessary contrast to each other. If everything were all light, you would not be able to see anything; likewise, if everything were all dark," said Sun. "One enhances the other, they need each other to have harmony, balance. Do you understand?" "I think so Sir, but I thought that dark things were bad," said River. "Have you seen my brother, The Night Dragon?" asked Sun. "Oh yes," answered River. "He flies by sometimes at night, I always hide under the water when I see him." "Why don't you call to him, he would be happy to speak with you," chided Sun. "I thought he might eat me, Sir," said River, hanging his head to hide his emotions. The Sun Dragon had a hard time hiding his amusement, and after a while he responded. "You thought that The Night Dragon goes around eating young dragons?" "That's what Rain told me, Sir" whispered River. "The Rain Dragon is only a few centuries older than you are, but you took his word for this bit of misinformation?" said Sun, steam visibly rising from his scales. "Yes Sir," said River, shaking at the awesome display of restrained dragon rage.

The Sun dragon drew a long breath, slowly regaining his composure. "If I dip my tail in this river, what will happen?" asked Sun. "The water will evaporate into steam, Sir," answered River. "Would that be a good thing?" asked Sun. "Oh no," said River "It would be very bad for the river and the things that live here!" He hoped The Sun Dragon would not damage his beloved river. "Yes, that would be bad," said Sun. "And I am almost entirely made of light. Do you see that light is capable of evil, just as much as dark is capable of good?" "I suppose it is," sighed River, beginning to get the point of The Sun Dragon's questions. "You mustn't be so swift to judge things, Young River. while it is true that some things are good, and some are not good, everything has the capacity to be both, no matter what they appear to be," said The Sun Dragon, in a deep quiet voice. "A dragon is wise enough to see past such things, and allow everything to exist on its own terms." "So, The Night Dragon is really a good dragon?" asked River. "Don't tell him that I said so, but I believe that the light he holds within him, may be more powerful than my own," whispered The Sun Dragon. "Next time he flies by, call out to him. I'm sure he will love to educate you on the power of contrast, and the beauty found in darkness."

The River Dragon thought that he might wait a few hundred years before calling The Night Dragon down for a chat, but he would never tell The Sun Dragon that. The Sun Dragon rose into the sky, circled, and flew off towards the west. The River Dragon sank to the muddy bottom of a deep pool, to cool off, and to think.

THE CLOUD DRAGON

Mother Cloud is a very prolific dragon, bearing more baby dragons than any other, in her long existence. She inhabits the sky, the land and the water. She visits all her children, and her children live in every part of the planet.

"There you are River. I have been looking for you," said Mother Cloud, in her soft whispering voice. "Hello Mother," replied River. "I have been sitting here meditating, for quite some time." "What are you meditating upon, that keeps you still for so long?" asked Cloud. "See how the water reflects the light?" said River, "It shimmers and dances, almost enough to blind you during the day, and resolves itself into quietly reflecting the moonlight at night." "I have observed this reflected light, my son. What is it that holds your interest so intently?" asked Mother Cloud. "Well, you see, the water has no light of its own, yet it can reflect it so intensely, like a mirror, and sometimes like it has a life of its own." said River. "Everything has a life of its own, dear one, and there is nothing wrong with reflecting the glorious light of others into the world," whispered Mother Cloud. "Not everything can be Dragon, after all"

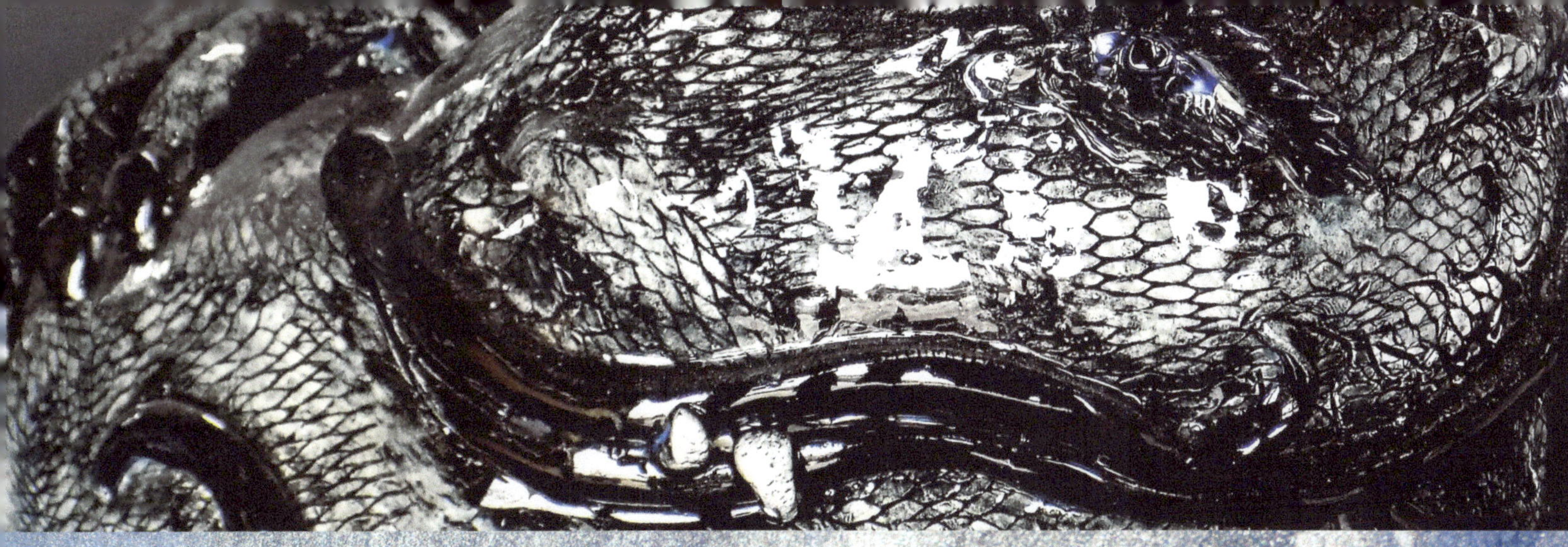

THE SMOKE DRAGON

Sometimes you can smell Smoke before you ever see him. His odor can be acrid and choking, or pleasant, like distant wood smoke. He has the ability to materialize suddenly, and to disappear just as quickly. His ability to come and go without visual approach sets him apart from other dragons, although his scent often gives him away, before he has time to appear.

"Hello Smoke," said The Night Dragon. It didn't matter that he couldn't see his friend, Night knew that smell well enough to be sure of Smoke's approach. "How are you, dear Night?" replied Smoke. "It is so dark and moonless that I almost passed this mountain top without spotting you." "I enjoy the blackness," replied Night. "What are you up to, my acrid friend?" "Oh, I'm just out to enjoy the air," said Smoke. Night let out a mighty laugh that filled the air with smoke of his own. "I had forgotten that you mated with Cloud, have the eggs hatched then?" "I fear to land, lest I step on one of the hatchlings, and crush it," said Smoke. "How many?" asked Night. "Three," answered Smoke. "They are wonderful, and awful, all at the same time." "Let us go for a hunt then, it will restore your nerves, and Cloud will love fresh food for your brood," said Night. They took off silently, into the blackness.

Shape Shifting

If I am as big as a mountain,

will you see me?

If I am as small as a fly,

will you take the opportunity to crush me?

If I stand before you with all the honesty I can muster,

will you accept me?

I await your notice,

look for me!

By, The River Dragon

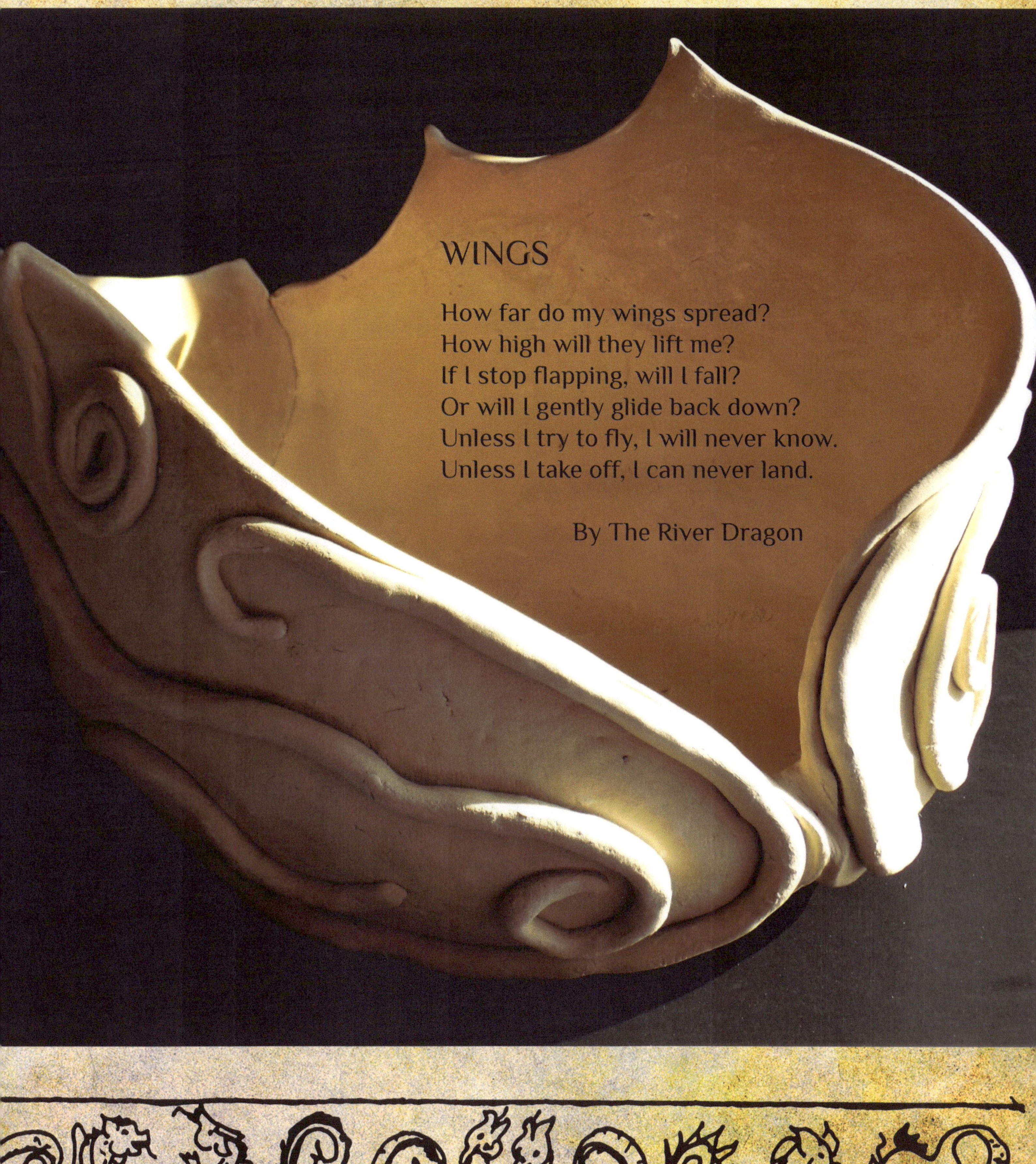

WINGS

How far do my wings spread?
How high will they lift me?
If I stop flapping, will I fall?
Or will I gently glide back down?
Unless I try to fly, I will never know.
Unless I take off, I can never land.

By The River Dragon

THE ICE DRAGON

Unlike most hot dragons, she has an icy core. Her scales shimmer with translucent, crystalline beauty. She seldom leaves the frigid realm of the northern polar ice cap. Her home is a large ice cave, surrounded by a frozen sea of floating icebergs. The Ice Dragon flies as well as she swims. She is revered for her ability to see all issues clearly and is sometimes called upon to mediate disputes, a rare occurrence in the dragon world.

ONE NIGHT THE CLOUD DRAGON CAME TO VISIT.

The Ice Dragon rose from the frigid sea, with her catch held in her icicle like teeth, to find The Cloud Dragon reclining in front of her cave. "Hello, Dear Cloud" said The Ice Dragon, "What a lovely surprise!" "Greetings Ice, how are you this fine evening?" responded Cloud. "It is your health I am concerned about, how is it that you are so far away from your hatchlings?" asked Ice. "Oh, dear Moon is watching them tonight," said Cloud. "I can ask for no better sitter than she." "Indeed, there can be nothing but peace with her in charge!" Both dragons chuckled, making a sound like wind chimes and bells. "I just came up here to cool off and get away from all of the commotion of my brood." said Cloud. "Of course," said Ice "We all need a break now and then." She nosed some fish in Clouds direction. "Here, have a snack, it must be exhausting keeping up with three babies at once. Do you have enough food in your larder?" asked Ice. "Oh, the larder is quite full, thank you." Cloud said as she crunched the nearly frozen fish in her mouth. "It seems every dragon on the planet has brought tribute to my young. I'm surprised there isn't some sort of famine because of it." Ice chortled at the thought of such hysteria, the entire planet of dragons visiting Cloud and her brood. "I'm not complaining, mind you." said Cloud, "They have all been wanting to help, especially Smoke and Night, the dear things. They bring food

almost every day." "Well, it is Smoke's duty to provide for his offspring, but Night is helping too? That is unexpected," said Ice. "That thought did cross my mind as well," said Cloud. "You would think they were his own." "Perhaps he seeks to foster one of them. Do you think that is his motive?" asked Ice. "That thought also crossed my mind," said Cloud. "Do you think that he would want to?" "What an interesting turn of events that would be!" said Ice. The two dragons sat in companionable silence, pondering the thought of The Night Dragon wanting to raise a young dragon! It was almost unheard of, at least it hadn't happened for many thousands of years. Night certainly had the knowledge and skills to pass on to a young dragon, but why would he commit to a thousand years of raising one?

After a while The Cloud Dragon rose to her feet, shook the snow from her scales and prepared to fly home. "Come again, dear Cloud, when you can get away, that is," said Ice. "I wish I could visit more often, Ice, but you know how it is with the brood to care for," said Cloud. "No one has hatched three babies at one time for at least 10,000 years, dear," said Ice. "If you need anything, just send out the word, every dragon on the planet is here for you." "I will remember that," said Cloud as she lifted off, creating a shower of snow and ice.

THE SUN DRAGON AND THE NIGHT DRAGON

The Sun Dragon was lounging in his favorite volcano, when he was hailed by The Night Dragon. "Hello brother," said Night, as he circled the lava pool. "How goes it with you?" "Brother!" replied Sun "I was hoping to see you." The Night Dragon landed delicately on the rim of the volcano. The Sun Dragon swam to the edge, to get his head closer to The Night Dragon. "Won't you join me dear brother?" asked Sun. "No thank you dear brother," replied Night. "The last time I bathed in lava, I had dried lava rock between my scales for days." "Humph," said Sun. "It just drips off of me." "Well, you are much hotter than I am, dear brother," said Night. "I shall stay here and breathe the sulfur fumes. Good for the lungs you know." "Good indeed" agreed Sun. "Now why is it that you were hoping to see me?" inquired Night. "Oh, no matter of urgency, but I thought it would be good to inform you of some news," said Sun.

The two dragons settled themselves, as if to take a firmer grip on the planet. "Well, come on brother, spit it out," said Night, at last showing an impatience that surprised himself. "It's nothing, really, dear Night, just some things I have heard, of late," said Sun, who wondered at the obvious tension in Night's demeanor. "I was speaking to young River a while ago, and he told me that his brother, Rain, had informed him that you make a habit of eating young dragons." "You mean the older, Rain, was frightening his younger brother with scary stories? How unusual, brother, I'm sure that we never engaged in such nonsense!" said Night as he shook with a good belly laugh. "Oh, I remember the wild games we played on each other, when we were new to the world," said Sun. "I don't think they mean any harm, but, you are the subject of their fun, and that is my concern." "What does it matter if River fears that I will eat him?" said Night. "Well, I have also heard that you are interested in fostering one of the triplets," said Sun. "And in that case, a reputation of eating young dragons will not serve you very well."

The Night Dragon went suddenly very still, as if he were about to pounce on some prey. The Sun Dragon swiveled his head to take in his brother's full length. The Night Dragon drew a long, slow breath and said, "Where did you get this information from?" "Is it merely idle female speculation then?" said Sun with a tone of disgust in his voice. "I thought my source was more reliable than that." "Well, I have been doing a lot of hunting for the brood," said Night. "It gives me an excuse to hunt for more than my share, and now that I think of it, the hatchlings are cute enough to eat, if you know what I mean." Sun laughed at his brother's joke, sending billows of smoke into the air. "So, it never even occurred to you to foster one of the triplets?" asked Sun. "Not once, until just now, when you mentioned it," said Night. The two dragons sat and looked at each other, they slowly broke into peals of laughter. The ground shook, smoke filled the air and anyone looking would have thought that the volcano was about to erupt.

When their mirth finally subsided, they sat wiping the tears from their eyes. Sun looked at Night with a sudden realization, and said "Do you think that this was their plan all along, to put the idea into your head? It will be a thousand years before any of the babies will be ready to foster. Were they planting a seed, so that it would be ready, when the time does come?" "Who gave you this information?" asked Night. "It was The Ice Dragon," said Sun. "From a conversation she had with Cloud herself. That's why I thought it to be true." "She would seem a reliable source," said Night. "She would, after all, be the one to arbitrate such a decision." "Yes," said Sun. "But was she planting the idea for future use, or did it come into the world of its own volition?" The Night Dragon pondered this possibility. "If this idea came into the world on its' own, then it might be a very powerful thing indeed." said Night "I'm not sure how it will turn out!" "Don't let it worry you, brother," said Sun. "We shall stand together, whatever the outcome." The Night Dragon rose and flew off to the west. The Sun Dragon shook the lava from his scales and flew to the east. Each of them knew that ideas could be powerful, especially if they come into the world on their own.

THE GATHERING

Once a year, all the dragons on the planet meet on Dragon Island. It is a meeting, a celebration, a thought collective, a mating ritual, a ceremony and this year a place for the naming of the hatchlings.

Dragons all have names, wonderful, powerful names. They are never spoken out loud. Hatchlings may have pet names that their parents give them, but their formal dragon names are only announced once, in a ceremony, to all the dragons at the gathering. They believe that to speak a dragon's true name can give you power over that dragon, and no dragon wishes to give their power away. Eventually, each dragon takes on its own public name, choosing for itself an element that it associates with, like Sun, Moon or Night. The preparations for the gathering take months, everyone looks forward to the event.

THE NIGHT DRAGON AND THE SMOKE DRAGON

The Night Dragon and The Smoke Dragon met on the hillside near the brooding cave. It had become their habit to meet there before the hunt.

"I think we should fly to the northern mountains tonight," said Night. "We have not hunted there for a long time." "That would be good," replied Smoke. "Better chance of finding some unsuspecting prey." "How is the name choosing coming then?" asked Night. "You only have a few weeks to come up with two names." "I am so glad that Cloud is naming the female," said Smoke. "I would never be able to come up with three perfect names. Hop is so much like me, I think I can use part of my own name for him, but Wiggle is so different, I have no idea what to do!" "Be glad that they will eventually choose their own name, and what cannot be spoken, will neither harm nor help them," said Night. "Still, I want to do my best," said Smoke. "They are my own, after all." "Of course," said Night. "Let us be off to the north." The two dragons rose silently into the air and vanished into the darkness.

THE SUN DRAGON PREPARES THE ISLAND

The Sun Dragon arrived at Dragon Island a few days early. He liked to spend time basking in the lava of the island's central volcano, and he thought he could lend a hand wherever there was a need. Already, the place was a hub of activity. The Day Dragon was, as usual, in charge of preparing the dancing grounds, a wide field, stretching from the beach to the base of the volcano. "Hello Day," said Sun. "How may I help you?" "Sun! I am so glad you're here!" exclaimed Day. "Would you be a dear and burn away the brush from the edges of the field? The jungle makes my dancing grounds smaller every year!" "Of course, my dear, I'll be happy to," said Sun. He circled the field, his tremendous heat igniting even the greenest brush, as if it were dry kindling. The Sun Dragon laughed as he made his way back to the Day Dragon. "That was fun, can I burn anything else down for you?" Day wrinkled her snout in thought. "I know, you are aware that The Sea Dragon is the mistress of ceremonies this year, I think that the sea platform will need to be made bigger, so that she can fit on it." "You want me to fly some boulders from the mountain down to the sea, to extend the stage?" asked Sun. "Perfect," said Day as she turned to tend to some other thing that needed her urgent attention.

The Sun Dragon began to wonder if he was as important to Day as he thought he was. No matter, he flew off to the summit of the volcano and began plucking large boulders and dropping them along the sea platform.

The Sea Dragon is the largest dragon on the planet, she would need at least twice as much space to fit her whole body upon.

When he had built up the rocks as much as he thought, necessary, he spotted The Ice Dragon coming out of the water. She walked over to the cave near the beach and deposited a large number of fish. The cave was already quite full of food, she then spewed an icy blast of water that froze everything in the cave into a large block of ice. Well, thought Sun, that should preserve the meat, even in this tropical heat. As Ice returned to the sea, he greeted her. "Well done, Ice, I thought all that prey might go to waste before everyone got here." "Hello, dear Sun," said Ice. "So good to see you." "It's good to see you too," replied Sun. "Are you staying on the island?" "I brought my own island this year," smiled Ice. "Look out there, about a mile off shore." Sun turned to the sea and saw a huge iceberg floating out past the waves. "How did you ever get that here?" he exclaimed. "The Sea Dragon and I pushed it," said Ice with a smile. Sun thought that it would take a dragon the size of Sea to push such a thing. "What a brilliant idea," said Sun. "Well, there are other cold loving dragons besides myself," said Ice. "Now we have comfortable accommodations. And Sea has made a lovely meeting grounds below the water, for all the water dragons to enjoy." "Everyone has outdone themselves this year," said Sun. "This shall be a gathering to remember."

ARRIVING

Dragons large and small began arriving on Dragon Island. As usual, everyone was delighted to see one another. Most dragons lead rather solitary lives, but they all treasure this yearly gathering, as a time to mingle and meet. The first days were filled with discussions, demonstrations, entertainments and stories. The Ice dragon set up a kind of court on her iceberg, to settle any disputes. There were only a few, and the dragons involved usually left on friendly terms.

When Cloud arrived with the triplets, everyone went wild with excitement. The three hatchlings had no idea what all the fuss was about, but they accepted the adoration as if it was their daily routine. Cloud set up the nursery in a cave, not far from the dancing grounds. She hoped that she could enjoy the festivities and keep track of her hatchlings.

THE NAMING CEREMONY

In the late afternoon, on the last day of the gathering, everyone met at the dancing grounds. The dragons formed a circle. The Cloud Dragon came into the center, nudging the female hatchling she had come to call Swirl ahead of her. The baby dragon twirled and somersaulted into the clearing. She was mostly white, like her mother, with pale pink stripes and tiny gauze-like wings. Cloud cleared her throat, the crowd went silent. "This is my flesh and my blood," said Cloud. "I claim the honor of naming her." Then Cloud let out a sound that can only be described as wind and bells, the very air vibrated with power and beauty. Every dragon present could feel the authority and grace that her name implied. The crowd of dragons bowed and murmured their approval of the name. No one would ever forget it. Cloud ushered Swirl to the edge of the clearing and Smoke strode into the center with the other hatchlings riding on his back. He put the one he called Hop into the center. Truly looking so much like his father, Hop was a dark grey smoke color. The baby, true to his nickname, hopped up and down, then, for a second he hovered slightly before landing. The crowd cheered at the sight.

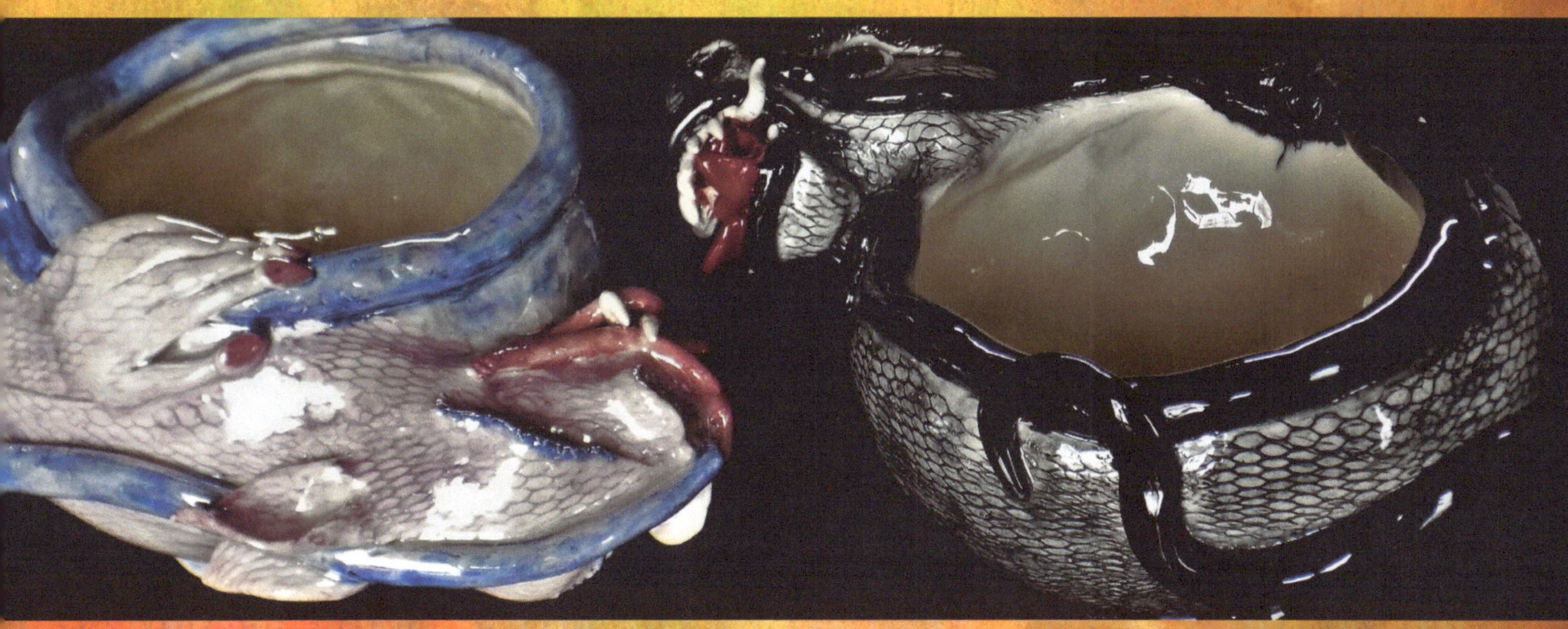

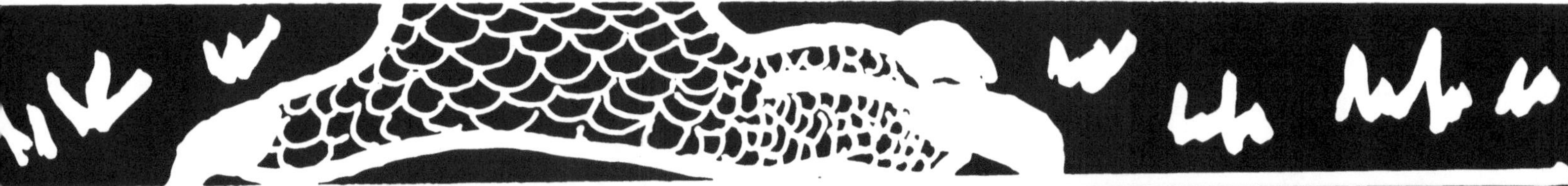

The Smoke Dragon cleared his throat, sending up a puff of black. "This is my flesh and my blood, I claim the honor of naming him." Then Smoke spewed out a long thin flame, followed by a reverberation of sound, like a large bronze gong and a roar, which came from deep inside of Smoke's chest. The crowd bowed and murmured their approval of the powerful name. Smoke had indeed used part of his own name, but added vibrations suggesting both wisdom and power. The hatchling strode over to his mother, holding his head high as if he had understood the blessing of his name.

Then Smoke put Wiggle into the center of the circle. The hatchling was black on top and white on the bottom, with large golden eyes. He walked in a small circle, then let out a small sneeze and to everyone's amazement, he disappeared. A few seconds later there was another small sneeze and the hatchling reappeared a few feet from his original position. The crowd cheered, no one could remember such a small dragon ever being able to disapparate before. Smoke looked at Cloud. Wiggle had never shown this ability before. He wondered how they would keep track of a disappearing hatchling! Smoke suddenly had an inspiration. He had worked out a name, but now he would add a new element to it. Smoke took hold of the hatchling's tail, lest he disapparate again, and said, "This is my flesh and my blood, I am honored to name him." Smoke let out a roar, which started and stopped, started and stopped, as if the name itself disapparated. It finally crescendoed into a loud, deep bell sound. The community of dragons roared back their approval and appreciation of the well-chosen name. Wiggle immediately hid between his father's legs. Smoke bowed to the crowed. Cloud came to join him in the center of the circle. The hatchlings peered out from underneath their parents' bellies.

A CELEBRATION

After all the congratulations wound down, the drumming began. The dragons once again formed a circle and The Day Dragon strode into the center. She began to sing and dance. Soon the crowd joined her, the drumming became wilder and so did the dancing. Dragons danced on the ground and in the air. Some songs were sung by individual dragons, and some were so popular that everyone joined in. The Sun Dragon danced with Day, after she had sung many songs. Together they rose into the air and danced circles around Dragon Island.

Food was brought out. Sun loved to taste all the exotic fare that was provided. He tried some long, squiggly delicacy brought by The Sea Dragon.

Everyone enjoyed the party, the food, the dancing and singing. The lagoon was filled with dancing water dragons. The iceberg, out at sea, literally bobbed up and down from all the dancing upon it.

RIVER HAS A CHANGE OF HEART

Cloud had ushered the hatchlings into the nursery cave after they had eaten their fill. Rain and River had been conscripted into hatchling sitting service, with the condition that no scary dragon stories were to be told. The Night Dragon himself agreed to tell them a bedtime story. It was a tale full of adventure, wonder and magic. River decided that The Night Dragon was not such a bad dragon after all, and vowed to himself to not take everything his big brother told him too seriously again.

SUN AND DAY

The merriment went on until sunrise. Dragons began to drift off, looking for comfortable places to sleep. The Sun Dragon and The Day Dragon took one more turn around the island, and settled themselves in the lava field near the top of the volcano to rest. "The party was excellent, Day" said Sun "You did a wonderful job this year." "I'm glad you enjoyed it Hot One," replied Day "You can help me clean up later, before we head home." "Of course, my dear, as soon as I have recovered my strength," said Sun. "Oh, I hope you haven't used up all your strength," said Day. "Not yet," said Sun as he slid close to The Day Dragon.

NIGHT AND RIVER

As the months passed, after the gathering, The Night Dragon found his eyes drawn more and more towards Wiggle. He wasn't sure what attracted him, but he started actively looking for the hatchling whenever he came with food, or if he came early, before the nightly hunt. The River Dragon also stopped often to see his young half-siblings. Cloud encouraged him to move to a nearby swamp, so that he could watch the hatchlings, while she was busy with other things. In exchange for his sitting services, River was also fed from the bountiful larder.

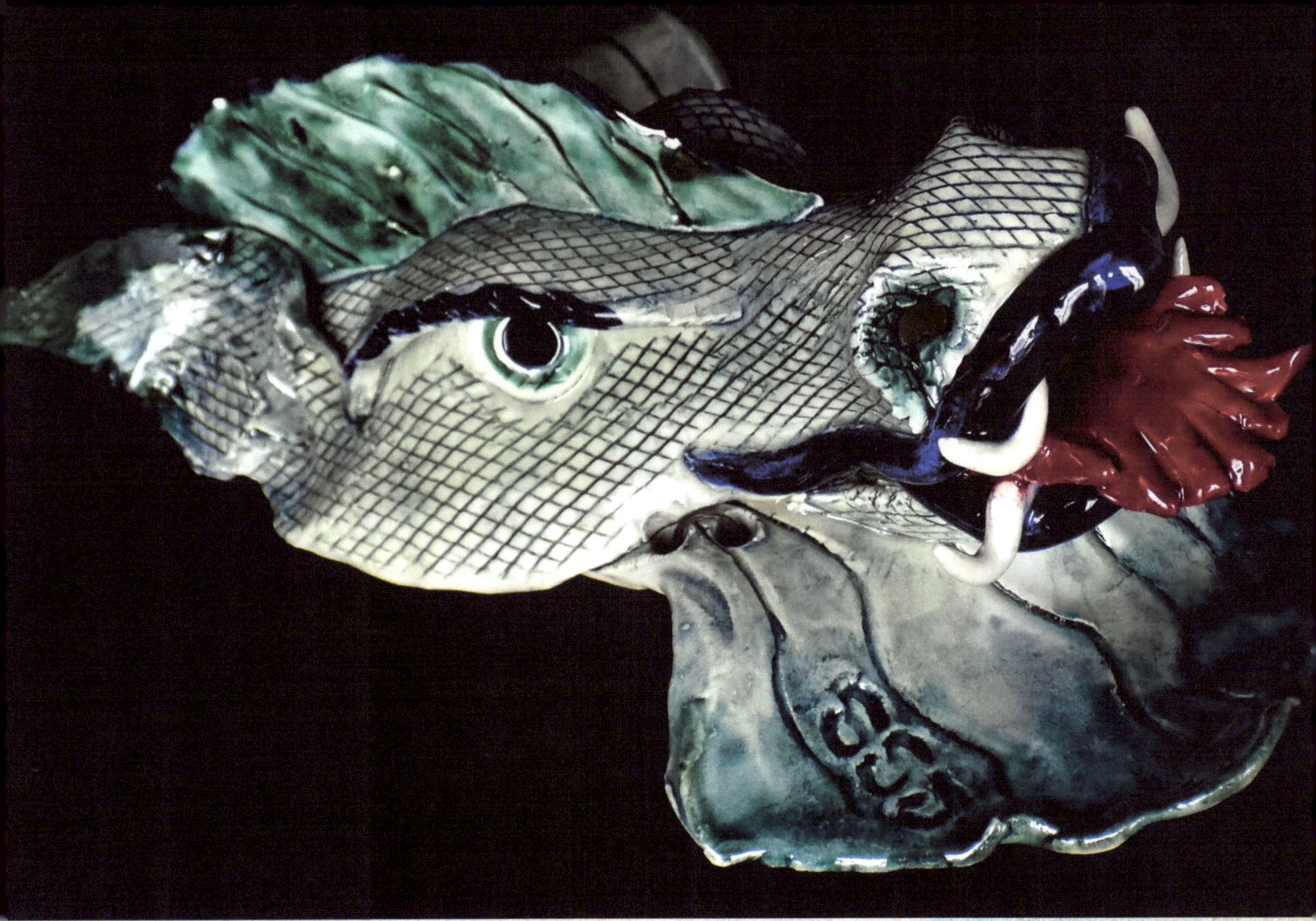

Some evenings, when there wasn't much need for more food, The Night Dragon and The Smoke Dragon would allow the young River Dragon to accompany them on the hunt. Other evenings River would beg The Night Dragon to tell the hatchlings a bedtime story. The triplets were too young to follow the stories very far, they usually fell asleep at the first lines spoken by Night's deep, resonant voice. River was the one who enjoyed The Night Dragon's stories. He loved listening to them; he would dream of being part of the tales in his sleep. He even day dreamed of taking part in the adventures and magic. As for The Night Dragon, he enjoyed telling tales and was somewhat flattered by River's rapt interest in them.

It occurred to The Night Dragon that he had no idea who River's father was. Why wasn't he training the young dragon in hunting skills? Why wasn't he telling him stories of his lineage and teaching him the ways of magic?

One evening, when they were alone, Night asked River if he knew of his father. "Young River," said Night, "I have told you about my own origins." "Yes Sir," replied River, "You and The Sun Dragon have been since the darkness and the light separated, when the world was first created." "That's right," said Night, "and your mother, The Cloud Dragon, was born when the water separated from the land, but I do not know who your father is, to tell you of his origins." "Oh," said River, "he is The Ocean Dragon, he lives in the deep ocean, on the other side of the planet." "The one where the Mer-people live?" asked Night "Yes, that's the one," said River. "Mother took me to see him once. He lives in a deep gorge at the bottom of the water. I went down with him, but it hurt my ears to go so deep under the ocean. I had to go back to the surface before I got to see very much." "It makes sense that you are descended from a water dragon," said Night "I don't know much about their ways, being a dragon of the air, myself." "I am a cross between air and water. That is why I choose to make my home in rivers, so that I can take advantage of both of my aspects," said River. "That is very wise of you," said Night, suddenly gaining a deeper respect for the young dragon. Not every dragon is so astute at his age. "How about if you teach me how to catch some fish tonight?" suggested Night. The River Dragon laughed "You will get all wet!" "I don't think it will hurt me much," said Night "I'll race you to the lake." They were both there faster than you could blink.

THE NIGHT DRAGON'S VISIT

The Night Dragon decided that he would go and visit The Ocean Dragon, to see what kind of dragon he was. Night had passed over this ocean, many times, but had seldom stopped to explore the area. He landed in early evening, on a rocky shoreline, where he had spotted mer-people in the past. He stood there, only a little while, when he was hailed by a mermaid, floating just off the shore. Night waded out into the placid water to speak with her. "Hello fair mermaid, how are you this fine evening?" asked Night. The mermaid responded in perfect Dragonese, "I am very fine, dark dragon, I hope you are not here to make a meal of me." "Not at all! I am The Night Dragon," he said with a bow. "I wish to speak with The Ocean Dragon, do you know him?" "Yes, I know him." replied the mermaid. "What is your business with him?" The Night Dragon was somewhat taken aback by her question. "Are you in his employ?" asked Night. "I assure you that this is a private matter between dragons." The mermaid laughed, "My father would never dream of paying me to direct strangers to speak with him. I think I would be banished from this ocean for asking for compensation."

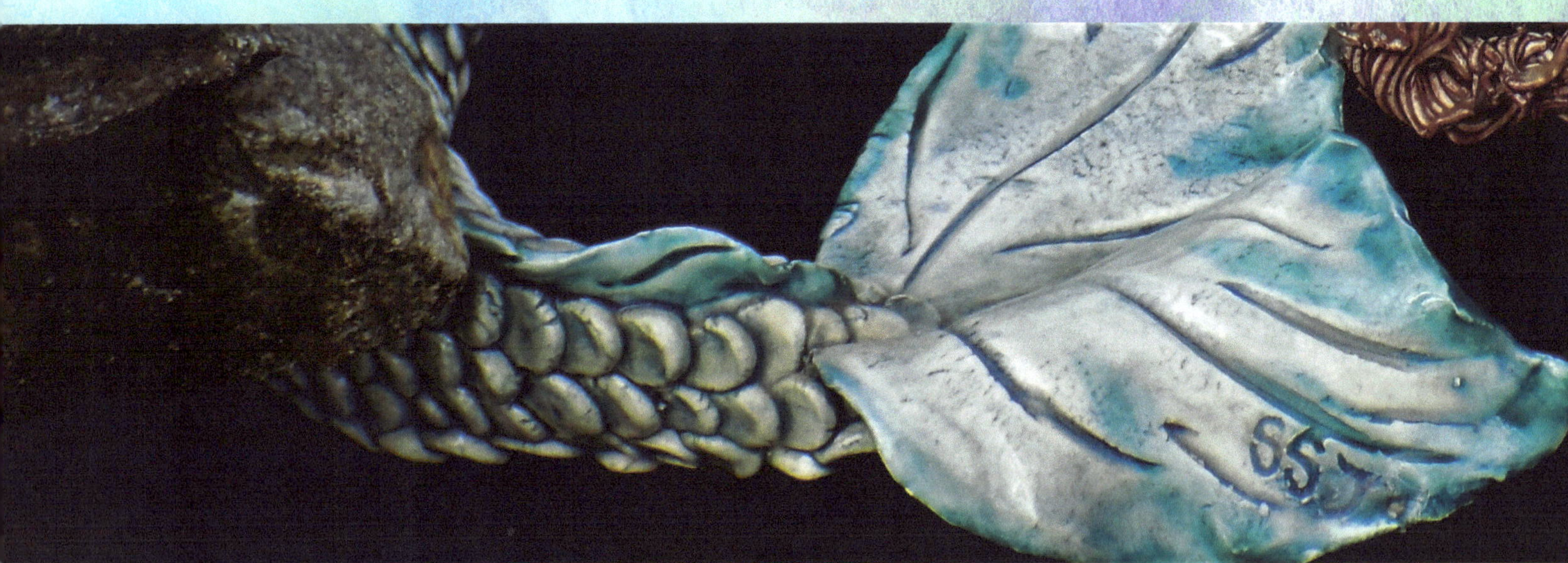

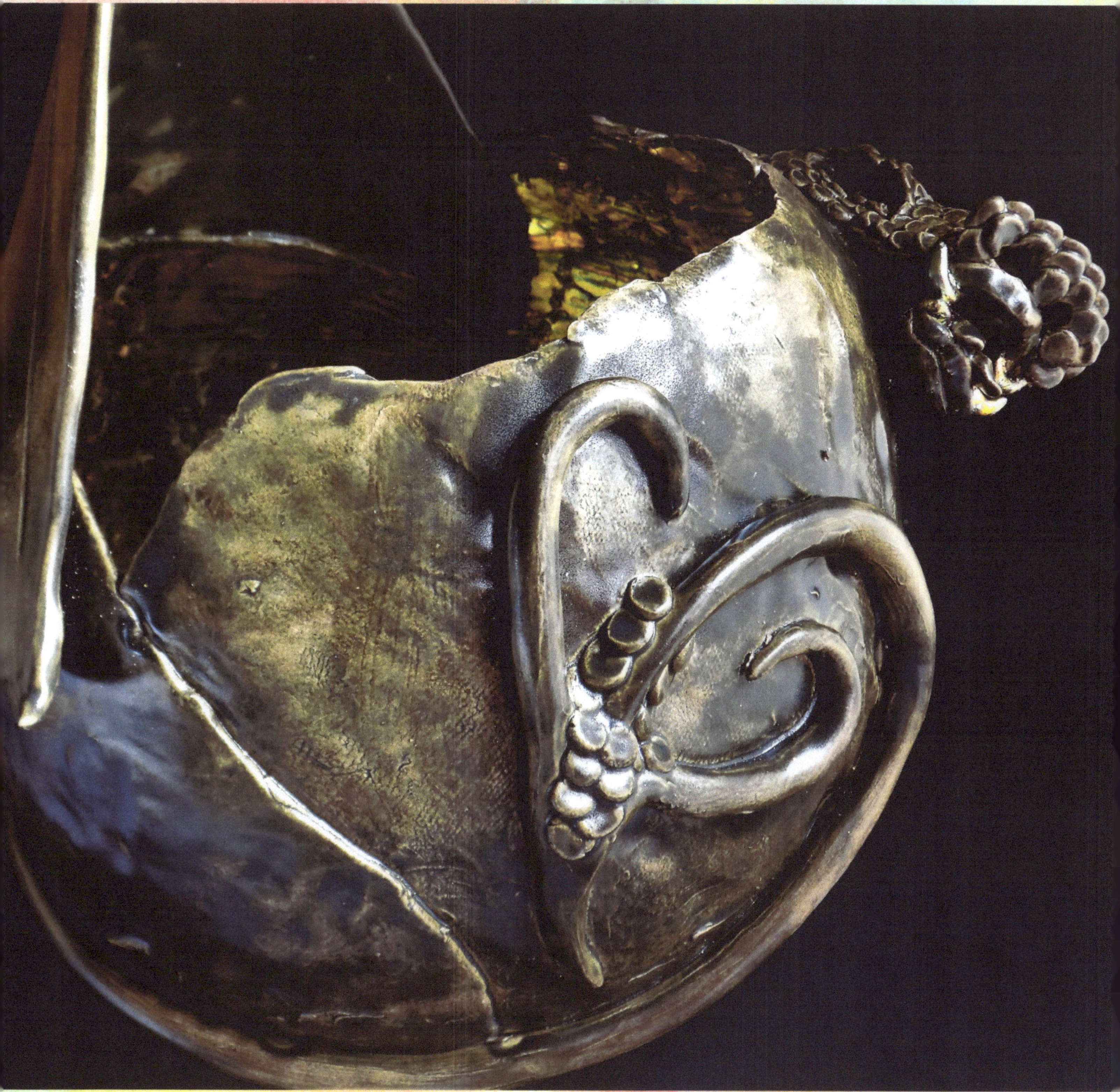

Now The Night Dragon was really taken aback. "How can he be your father?" he said, with more confusion in his voice than he wanted to show. She laughed again, and rose into the air, displaying the most wondrous pair of dragon wings he had ever seen. "I am both mermaid and dragon, as you can see," said the mermaid, who was indeed the most beautiful creature The Night Dragon had ever encountered. He was in fact immediately smitten by her beauty and grace, feeling like the world were somehow spinning faster, and out of control. He had never felt this way in all the eons of his existence. She flew a bit higher and then dove gracefully back into the water. Night felt suddenly crushed, as if his heart would break if he didn't see her again at once. She popped her head back out of the water and said, "I will inform The Ocean Dragon that you are here." She smiled and dove once more beneath the surface.

Night moved back to the beach. If this dragon lived in the deepest part of this ocean, it would be a while before he would surface. The Night Dragon tried to collect himself. 'You have seen beautiful things before. What is so special about this one, that has you so flustered?' he thought. 'Well, for one thing, you had no idea that a mermaid and a water dragon could mate and produce offspring! Such beautiful offspring,' he thought with a sigh. He tried to concentrate on what he would say to The Ocean Dragon, but his thoughts kept circling back to the mermaid. Merdragon? He wondered what she called herself.

THE OCEAN DRAGON

Suddenly there was a great rushing of water, and fountains of spray came from the sea. In a very dramatic fashion, The Ocean Dragon rose from the water, and glided to the edge of the beach, on a wave that proceeded to drench The Night Dragon as it hit the rocky shore. The Night Dragon allowed the water to drip off, refusing to shake himself to get rid of the wetness in front of this bold dragon. The Ocean Dragon bowed slightly, "I am here, what do you wish to see me about, Night Dragon?" "It is a pleasure to meet you, Ocean Dragon," said Night, with a bow, straining to maintain his politeness. "I have come to speak with you about your son, The River Dragon." The Ocean Dragon frowned. "Who? Oh, yes, one of Cloud's sons, what of him? He can only be about 500 years or so old, is he in some sort of trouble?" asked the Ocean Dragon.

"No trouble," replied Night. "I am a friend of The Cloud Dragon and The River Dragon. I thought it would be prudent to become acquainted with the youth's father, as well." "I thought she had taken up with some smoke dragon, and they had gone about populating the world with baby dragons," said Ocean. Night smiled, "Well, they have produced three hatchlings, not quite enough to fill the world. I have been spending time with Young River, since his mother is occupied with the hatchlings, and wondered why he was not being looked after by his father." "Does he need looking after?" asked Ocean, in a rather condescending tone. "He is old enough to take care of himself, is he not?" "River has been taking care of himself, and there is another 500 years before he will be ready to be formerly tutored in Dragon Ways, but he needs a male dragon role model to bring him into his full potential," said Night "I see you are powerful, here in your ocean, do you not wish that your son becomes powerful in his own right?"

The Ocean Dragon took a long moment to answer. "You see that I live here in this deep ocean. River is part water dragon and part air dragon, he cannot survive where I live and I cannot survive where he lives. Perhaps I should not have mated with Cloud, but when I saw her hovering in the sky, I had to know her. She is so beautiful, so... fluffy, like seafoam and mist. I'm afraid my heart took over my judgment. We have two sons you know, and I cannot live with either of them." Night thought of his recent encounter with Ocean's daughter, and knew exactly what The Ocean Dragon meant. "I understand your problem, and that is why I have come. I wish to ask your permission to work with River, and to perhaps foster him, when the time comes." The Night Dragon had not intended to ask this, but he had said the words, and what a dragon speaks from the heart becomes real, as soon as it is spoken. "You are very bold, Night Dragon," said Ocean. "I do not understand your motives, but I see that you are sincere in your words. I have many offspring and cannot possibly raise them all. You have my blessing to assist Cloud with the nurturing of our son, The River Dragon." The Ocean Dragon bowed formally, signifying the resolve of his declaration. The Night Dragon bowed in return. "Thank you for the honor. I will do my best with him."

"Please join me in some refreshments before you leave." said The Ocean Dragon. He slapped his long tail on the water, and immediately several mermaids appeared bearing large shells, laden with exotic fare. The Merdragon flew with them to the shore and deposited the food in front of Night. Once again, Night was awed by her beauty. "This is my daughter, Icthianna," said Ocean. She smiled and bowed formally to Night. "I am honored to meet The Dragon of the Night." Night thought that he would melt, or explode, but managed to say, "The honor is all mine, fair one." She then flew back to the ocean. Night knew he would never be the same again.

After tasting many unusual and delicious foods, Night bowed to Ocean, and flew into the dark sky.

NIGHT SEEKS SUN

As Night traveled to the west, he wondered why he had asked to foster River. It had never occurred to him to do any such thing. He thought that one day he might foster Wiggle, but that was a long time off, and he was not sure that it would even be necessary. River did need him though, and he was sure that he would be a good influence on the young dragon. Perhaps he should talk to Sun about this new turn of events, then he should speak with Cloud. He landed on a mountain top, and waited for morning to arrive.

As it turned out, Night met The Day Dragon shortly after morning came. "Hello, Night, I am surprised to find you here," said Day, as she landed delicately on the rocky ledge that Night was perched upon. "Hello Day," replied Night. "I am waiting here in hopes of spotting my brother." "Oh, well, I am meeting him at the granite hills, on the far side of this mountain," said Day. "Fly with me and we shall greet him together." "I was hoping to speak with him alone, if you don't mind, Day," said Night. "I will hunt us up some breakfast while you brothers chat," said Day. "Thank you, Day," said Night with a sigh of relief. The two dragons flew off toward the granite hills.

The Sun Dragon flew in from the south, shortly after Night and Day had arrived. Pleasantries were exchanged, and Day excused herself to hunt. "Well, what is it brother?" asked Sun. "You never seek me out unless you have something on your mind." The Night Dragon took a deep breath, and told the whole story, from beginning to end. Tears of mirth rolled down The Sun Dragon's cheeks, and sizzled for a second, before they evaporated completely. "Don't say it, even if it's true," said Night, seeing his brother holding back his laughter. "Don't say that my brother is the most caring, loving, light-filled, powerful beast that l have ever seen?" said Sun. "l don't feel very powerful at the moment," replied Night. "l feel slightly unhinged." "Oh, that's just the spell of the merdragon you spoke of." said Sun, giving his brother a little jab in the shoulder. "You are smitten with her. l didn't know such a being even existed." "l wondered about that too," said Night. "It surely has to do with a combination of dragon and mer- magic," said Sun. "She must be a magical creature indeed!" "The most wondrous, magical thing l have ever seen," said Night, shaking his head in awe.

"And you, fostering Young River!" said Sun. "I didn't see that coming!" "Neither did I," replied Night. "I didn't know until the words tumbled out of my mouth." "Well, they have been spoken now, so they must be honored," said Sun. "A dragon's words are sacred bonds." "Oh, I intend to keep my word," said Night. "I really do think that Young River needs someone to guide him. I just never thought that it would be me." "Then what is your hesitation? You should be celebrating," said Sun. "You are right, brother, I will speak with Cloud and River, and then we shall all celebrate," said Night, with a much happier countenance than he had started with.

Day arrived with a large catch of assorted prey. "Did I hear that you are celebrating something?" she asked, after depositing breakfast on the ground between them. The Sun Dragon filled her in on the details, while Night tried not to look embarrassed. Thankfully, Sun left out the part about Night being in love with The Merdragon. They ate their breakfast and Night flew off to speak with Cloud.

After Night departed, Sun told Day about The Merdragon, Icthianna. "I know her!" said Day. "We sometimes sing together on the rocky oceanside cliffs." "Well, of course, beauty knows beauty," said Sun. "How could it be otherwise?" "She is delightful," said Day. "You will love her." "If my brother loves her, it is enough for me," said Sun.

The Night Dragon flew to the nursery cave. As he landed, he spotted Cloud, curled up at the entrance. She looked up at him, slightly perplexed by the daytime appearance of The Night Dragon. 'He is resplendent in the sunlight,' she thought. 'But what could bring him here at this hour?' She hoped that there was nothing amiss. She scanned all her children with her inner knowing. 'Nothing wrong there,' she thought. 'What could it be?' Night bowed, somewhat formally, as he landed. "Hello, fair Cloud, how are you this fine morning?" said Night. Cloud took a moment before saying, "Very well indeed, dear Night, what brings you out on this sunny day?" Night found that he had to clear his throat before he could speak. "I wish to speak with you, dear Cloud, on a private matter." "You may speak freely Night, we are alone, except for the hatchlings inside the cave," said Cloud. "Well," started Night, "I was recently speaking to The Ocean Dragon, and we were discussing his role in raising Young River, or more specifically, his inability to instruct him." "Really!" replied Cloud, wondering how that meeting had come about. "And what was the conclusion of this discussion?" "The conclusion was that I volunteered to foster Young River, if you will permit it, of course." said Night. He found himself holding his breath, and let it out slowly.

Cloud's eyes opened wide, this was quite unexpected. "River is only 500 years old, he is not eligible to foster for another 500 years. He is barely beyond a hatchling himself!" "I seek only to teach him informally, until he is of age," responded Night. "I believe he could use the influence of an adult male dragon." "Well, I am grateful to you and Smoke for taking him hunting; I have always known that his father would not have much contact with him," said Cloud, her mind whirled with such surprising thoughts. She remembered her discussion with The Ice Dragon. They had thought that Night would seek to foster one of the triplets, not River. She had been content to let the matter rest for a thousand years, and then worry about it! Knowing that Night could not formally foster River for another 500 years was some solace. "I suppose you could spend time with River informally, until he is of age," said Cloud "We will see if it is appropriate for a formal declaration, when the time comes." "I am content with that," said Night, feeling somewhat relieved. "Thank you, Cloud." The Night Dragon bowed again and rose into the air. He thought his next mission might be even more difficult than this one.

He found River floating in the swamp, not far from the nursery cave. "Hello, Young River." said Night. "Night!" exclaimed River. "What are you doing here? I mean, greetings Great Night Dragon. Welcome to my swamp," he said in his best imitation of dragon courtesy. Night laughed. "I have come to speak with you, Young River." River wondered what he could have done wrong, to warrant a daytime visit from The Night Dragon. This was the first time he had seen Night in full daylight; he was startled to see how magnificent he was, sparkling in the light, like he was made from brown, blue and black crystals. River could almost see light radiating from within him. "I am honored by your visit, sir." The Night Dragon sat on a less boggy part of the swamp and turned to face Young River. "I have been given permission by your parents to begin informally training you in the ways of The Dragons." "You have spoken to my father?" asked River, astonished by the thought. "Yes," said Night "and your mother. We agree that you would benefit from a male dragon's influence, and since your father dwells in the depths of the ocean, I have volunteered to guide you until you are of fostering age."

River sat for a moment, pondering what this could mean. He decided that he had no idea. "What does this mean?" he asked. "It means that you get to hang out with me and learn how to be a great dragon," replied Night, with a wink. "Really?" said River. He could imagine nothing better in the whole world. Night laughed and splashed some swamp water in River's direction, with his tail. "The first thing we have to do is find you a better place to live!" "OK," said River. "Do I get to live with you?" "Only if you want to," replied Night "I don't have a formal home you know, just a few caves here and there where I keep my things."

River rose into the air and shook the swamp mud off his scales. "I'm ready when you are." Night rose as well. "Let's go somewhere less bright, all this sunlight hurts my eyes." They flew off together, towards the west.

Later, Day and Cloud had their heads together, making plans. "We should get The Sea Dragon to tell all the water dragons of our plans," said Day. "Yes, I will go and talk to her," said Cloud. "But without River around to watch the hatchlings, I must see if Smoke is available to watch the triplets." "Where is River?" asked Day. "Off with Night. I'm not sure where they went, but they flew away several hours ago," said Cloud. "It's nice that Night didn't waste any time starting his mission," laughed Day. The Smoke Dragon suddenly appeared in front of the nursery cave. "Hello ladies, how are you this fine day?" he said with a bow. "What's all this scuttlebutt about River moving out of the swamp?" "How did you hear about that?" asked Cloud. "I was sleeping by the water, and all the fish started singing about the departure of The River Dragon from their home," mused Smoke. "I couldn't get a wink of sleep!" All three dragons chuckled at the thought of the fish party a dragon's departure can cause. "They don't appreciate our presence," said Day. The females filled Smoke in on the details of the celebration plans thus far. "I'll be glad to watch the three little devils, my dear," said Smoke. "I will lie down and they can climb on me." "That will keep them entertained for a few minutes," said Cloud. "You had better plan on feeding them when they wake up from their nap, or they might chew your leg off!" "Don't worry, my dear," said Smoke "I've watched our little darlings before, and I still have all my fingers and toes!" "Well then, I shall go inform The Ice Dragon," said Day. "And I shall go visit Sea," said Cloud. They rose into the air and flew off in different directions.

Night and River flew to the dark side of the planet, and landed in a desert. "Do you want me to live here, in a desert?" asked River, who didn't like the idea of not having any water nearby. "No, I just wanted to show you something." said Night "See this cave over here, this is where I keep my books." "What books?" asked River. "I have a collection from all over the universe," said Night. "How do you get them here?" asked River. He had seen a few books that Cloud kept in the nursery, but he had no idea how to use them. "Magic mostly," said Night. "Some of the stories that I have told you have come from them." River loved the stories that Night told, full of marvelous adventures and strange lands. He had wondered how Night knew so many; he thought that The Night Dragon just made them up. "How do you use these books?" asked River. "Let's go in and I'll show you." replied Night.

When Cloud found The Sea Dragon, she was floating majestically in the middle of a group of tropical islands. With her wings out like giant sails, she was using the island breezes to propel herself across the turquoise waters. "Hello, Sea," shouted Cloud, from above The Sea Dragon's head. Sea lifted her eyes to the sky. "Cloud, what a pleasant surprise, what brings you here on this fine day?" Cloud deftly landed a few feet away from the enormous Sea Dragon. "I came to speak with you!" she said as she began to tread water. "Wonderful," said Sea. "Fill me in on all the news, I haven't seen another dragon since the gathering."

Cloud filled Sea in on all the details of the day and of the plans to celebrate Night's new arrangement with River. "That's the most extraordinary thing that I have ever heard," chuckled Sea "Of course we should celebrate this great event! When shall this all take place?" "We plan to have it on Dragon Island, but I don't think we have a day set," said Cloud. "Why not do it on the solstice?" said Sea. "There are a few weeks yet to prepare, and it is an auspicious time to come together and celebrate." "What a wonderful suggestion!" said Cloud "The dragons haven't gotten together at solstice for eons!" "Then it is time," said Sea.

Cloud and Sea decided to go to Dragon Island to see what needed to be done to prepare the place. Cloud flew and Sea swam under the water (her fastest mode of travel). As The Sea Dragon rose out of the water, she said to Cloud, who was already on the beach, "I will travel to visit my brother, The Ocean Dragon, and make arrangements for all interested parties to attend." "Do you think you can persuade your brother to come?" asked Cloud "and what about The Merdragon?" "I will do my best to persuade the entire ocean to attend," Sea said with a jolly laugh. Cloud knew how persuasive Sea could be. She was quite eloquent as mistress of ceremonies at the gathering. They made a mental list of things to prepare, and went on their appointed missions.

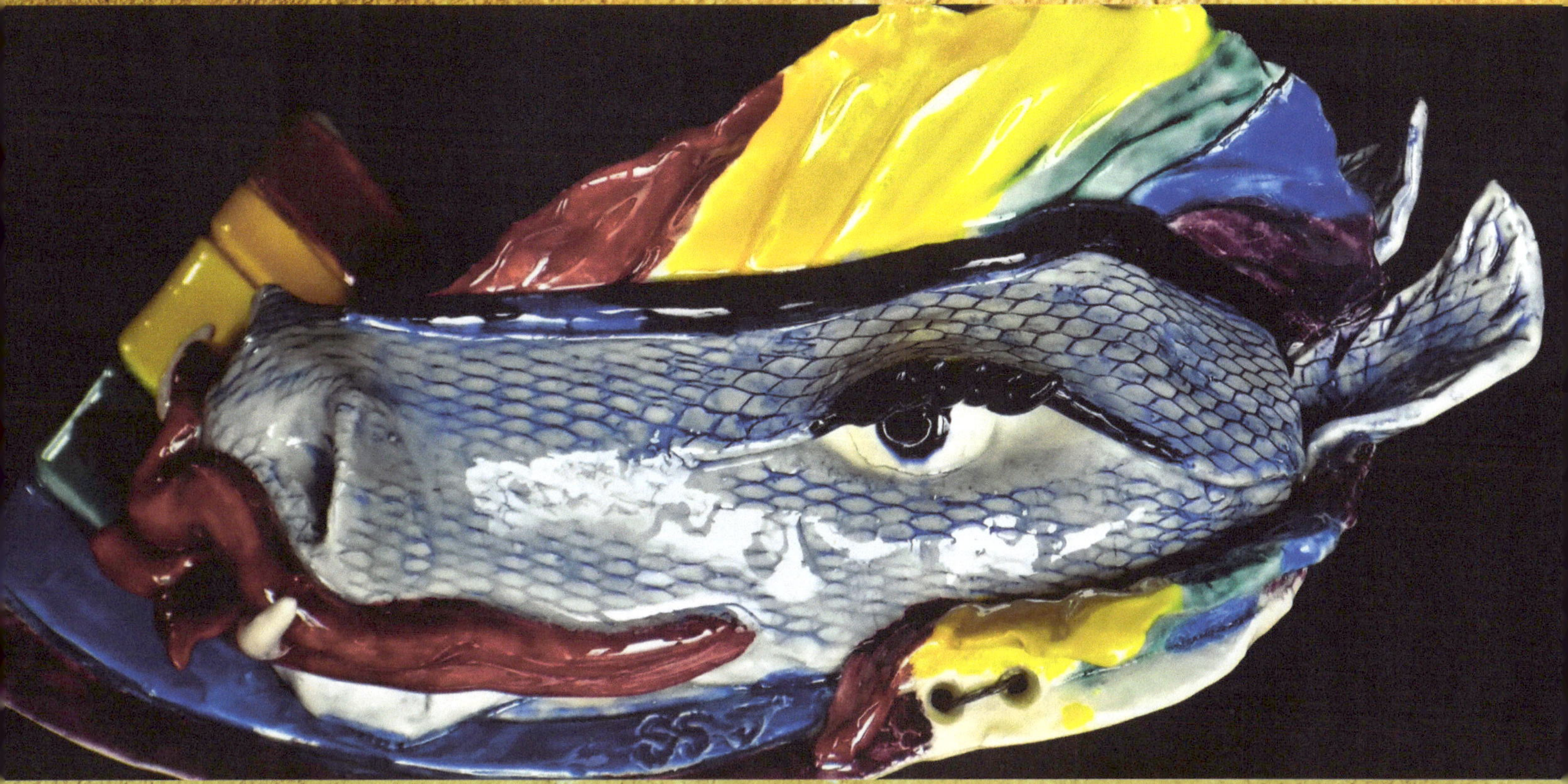

When Cloud returned to the nursery cave, she found Day basking in the hot springs near the entrance. "How did your meeting with Ice go?" "Great, Ice is creating an official commendation for all the parties involved," said Day. "She thinks that more dragons need to be concerned about our young, and their educations." "I really hadn't considered the political implications of all this," said Cloud. Once again, she had the feeling that more was going on than it seemed. "You look positively blue, dear. Was it cold up there?" "Some sort of blizzard. Ice was ecstatically rolling in the snow as I arrived. Not a place for heat-loving dragons like myself." said Day. "Well, if we all took to the same climate, we would be living on top of each other," laughed Cloud. "Oh, I'm very glad that we dragons spread out to use all the climates our planet has to offer." said Day, as she dipped her head under the steaming water.

That evening, River and Night arrived at the nursery bearing a large catch of prey. Strange and exotic prey by the look of it. "Where in the world have you two been?" asked Cloud. "Everywhere, Mother," said River with such a satisfied look about him that Cloud had to laugh. "I guess that means you've enjoyed your day with your new mentor." "Oh, yes! Night is the best tour guide ever!" said River. "Tour guide?" asked Cloud, with a look at The Night Dragon. "I told him we would start with a tour of the planet," said Night, "I think it went rather well, don't you?" He pointed at their exotic collection of prey. "What's that around your neck, River?" asked Cloud. "It is a holder for books," said River. "Night let me borrow some from his library cave." Cloud once again gave Night a long look. "Are you planning to teach him to read already?" "Only in one or two languages, Cloud, nothing too strenuous, I assure you," said Night, with a wink aimed at River. "The youth's mind needs stimulation if he is to become a great thinker."

"River, you go inside and play with the triplets, while l store all of this catch in the larder," said Cloud "l would like a few minutes alone with Night, too." River went into the cave and Cloud turned to Night. "l hope you know what you're getting yourself into here." "l think l have a good grasp of the situation," said Night. "l don't mind spending time with the lad." "Yes" said Cloud. "lt all seems innocent enough, but my intuition keeps telling me that there is more going on here than any of us can see." "ls that a bad thing?" asked Night "l too have felt that there are powers at work beyond our knowing, but l feel no malice in it. Perhaps we are to do something greater than we intend." "Whatever could that be?" said Cloud. "l think we will just have to wait and see," said Night. He bowed to Cloud. "Tell River that l will return tomorrow evening. He'll need some rest for our next adventure." With that, he flew off into the growing darkness.

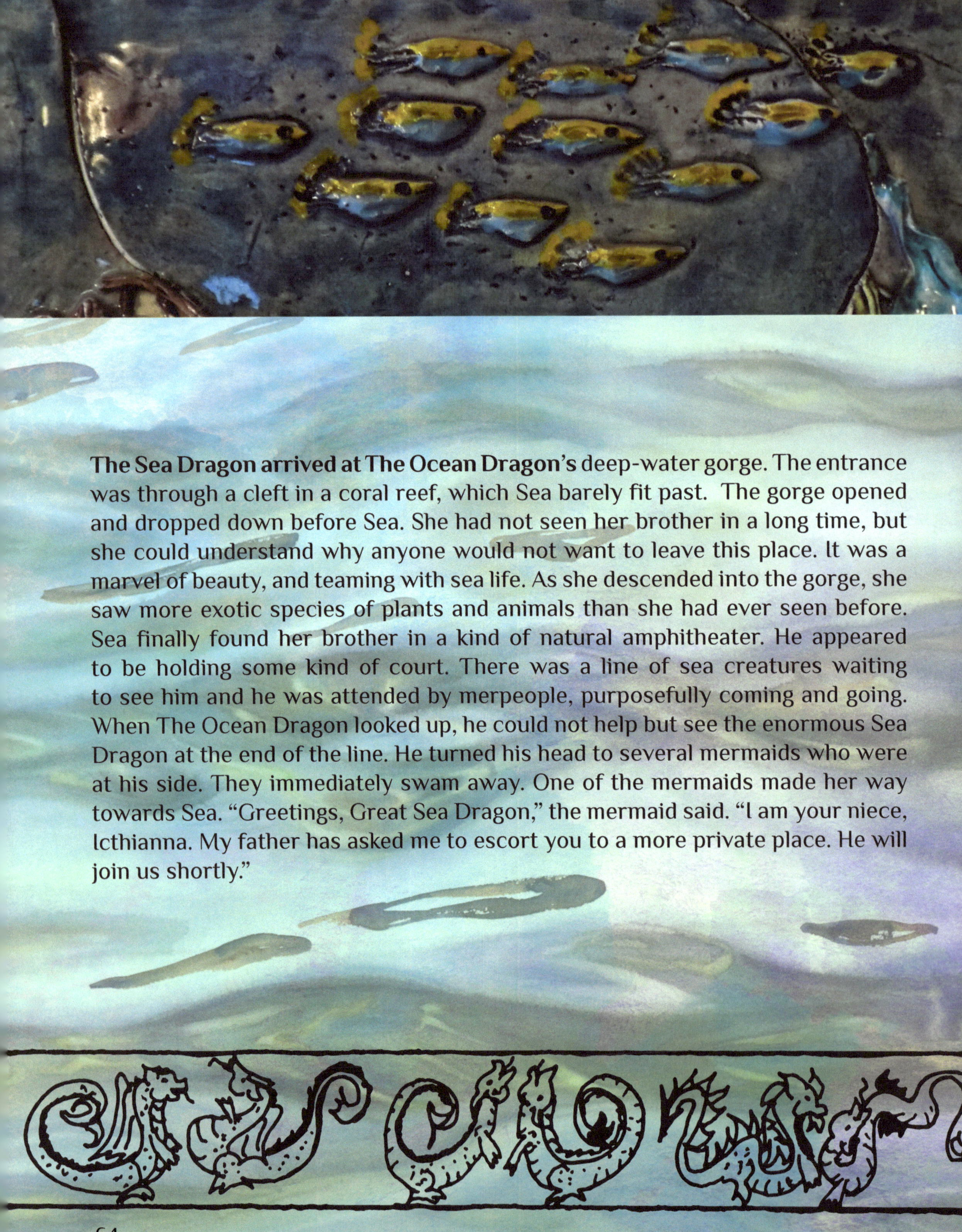

The Sea Dragon arrived at The Ocean Dragon's deep-water gorge. The entrance was through a cleft in a coral reef, which Sea barely fit past. The gorge opened and dropped down before Sea. She had not seen her brother in a long time, but she could understand why anyone would not want to leave this place. It was a marvel of beauty, and teaming with sea life. As she descended into the gorge, she saw more exotic species of plants and animals than she had ever seen before. Sea finally found her brother in a kind of natural amphitheater. He appeared to be holding some kind of court. There was a line of sea creatures waiting to see him and he was attended by merpeople, purposefully coming and going. When The Ocean Dragon looked up, he could not help but see the enormous Sea Dragon at the end of the line. He turned his head to several mermaids who were at his side. They immediately swam away. One of the mermaids made her way towards Sea. "Greetings, Great Sea Dragon," the mermaid said. "I am your niece, Icthianna. My father has asked me to escort you to a more private place. He will join us shortly."

The Sea dragon looked closer and saw that this was The Merdragon she had heard about from Cloud. "I am pleased to meet you, niece, part of my mission has to do with you." Icthianna seemed undisturbed by this news, she smiled and waved her arm. "This way Auntie, we can speak privately in here." They swam to the mouth of a cave. "Is there room for me in there?" asked The Sea Dragon. "Oh, it is bigger than it looks, once you are inside," said Icthianna. As The Sea Dragon pushed her head through the opening, she saw that it was indeed a huge, cavernous sea cave, decorated, furnished and currently full of mermaids, scurrying about with giant shells full of food. Icthianna turned to Sea and said, "Come on in Auntie, there is room enough for you." Sea entered and settled herself along a large wall. "This is nice," said Sea, "Is this where Ocean sleeps?" "Yes, and about 100 of his servants and some of his offspring," replied Icthianna. "Servants?" asked Sea, "Why does he need servants?" "Everyone is well-paid and very happy to work for The Ocean Dragon," said Icthianna, "We live a very harmonious life here." "I see," said The Sea Dragon, not really understanding what her brother was doing, but somewhat reassured that her niece claimed to be happy.

"What is it that you wished to speak to me about?" asked Icthianna. "You are invited to a party," said Sea. "Everyone who is interested may come, but I extend this invitation to you specifically upon the request of The Cloud Dragon, and The Day Dragon." "Oh, yes" said Icthianna. "I know The Day Dragon, she sometimes stops and sings with me, and isn't The Cloud Dragon the mother of my half-brothers, Rain and River?" "Yes, that's correct," said Sea. "We would all like you to attend, so that we may know you better." Before Icthianna could respond, The Ocean Dragon entered the cave. "Dear Sea! How wonderful to see you! What brings you to my humble domain?" "My dear brother," said Sea, "Your domain is anything but humble, it is extraordinary!" "Thank you my dear," replied Ocean, "To what do I owe this visit?" "There is to be a party," said Sea, "on Dragon Island, to celebrate the new relationship between The Night Dragon and The Young River Dragon."

"What has that to do with me?" spouted Ocean. "River is your son," said Sea, "You cannot ignore your responsibility for the raising of your offspring." "I am surrounded by my offspring!" said Ocean, with a glance towards Icthianna. "Now you want me to attend a party to celebrate giving my parenting privilege to another dragon?" "I don't see that you are giving anything away," said Sea. "You are assuring that your son will be raised as a proper dragon." "By another!" spouted Ocean, "They can celebrate without me!" The Sea Dragon looked at her brother and saw the hurt in his eyes. She took a long breath, "I know that you would rather not be embarrassed by admitting that you can't offer River your own wisdom, but let's be practical here. Night is more than capable of educating River in dragon ways. Cloud, poor thing, is busy with three hatchlings, and you live at the bottom of the ocean, a place where Young River cannot go."

"Must l admit my short-comings to all of Dragondom?" sighed Ocean. "You were the one who mated with a dragon of the air," said Sea. "You must look at this as an opportunity to do what is best for Young River. Show all the other dragons that education of our youth is more important than your pride. Take this chance to be the bigger dragon, little brother." The Ocean Dragon looked up at his sister. "You are very persuasive Sea, l should ask you to stay and help rule my domain." "As lovely as it is, l have a sea of my own, brother. Just come to Dragon lsland and give your blessing to the arrangement. You could use some time away." "Alright, tell my daughter, when and she can rearrange my schedule so that l can be there," said Ocean. "l have been invited too, father," said lcthianna. Ocean lifted an eye towards his sister. Sea smiled at Ocean. "Very well, you and all your half-siblings may go. You make all the arrangements," he said. "Oh, thank you father!" lcthianna hugged Ocean, then Sea, then quickly swam out of the cave. "l didn't even ask that you send the rest of your offspring to the celebration," said Sea. "But you would have gotten around to it eventually," said Ocean, "l just thought l would save you the trouble, sister. Here, have something to eat, you must be famished."

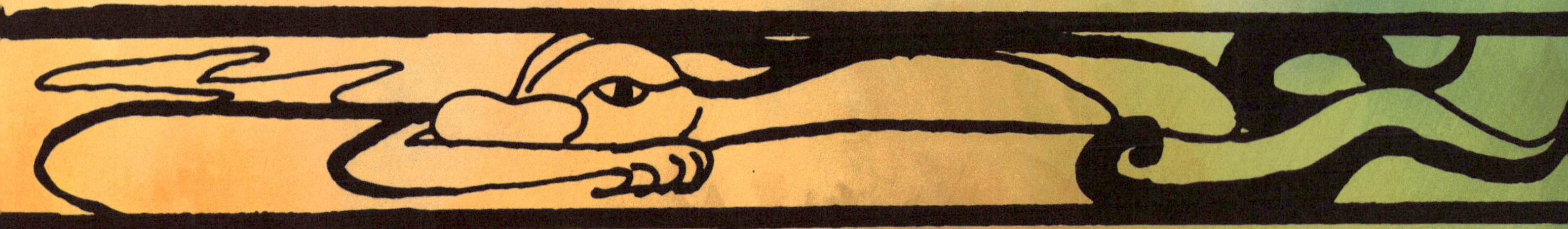

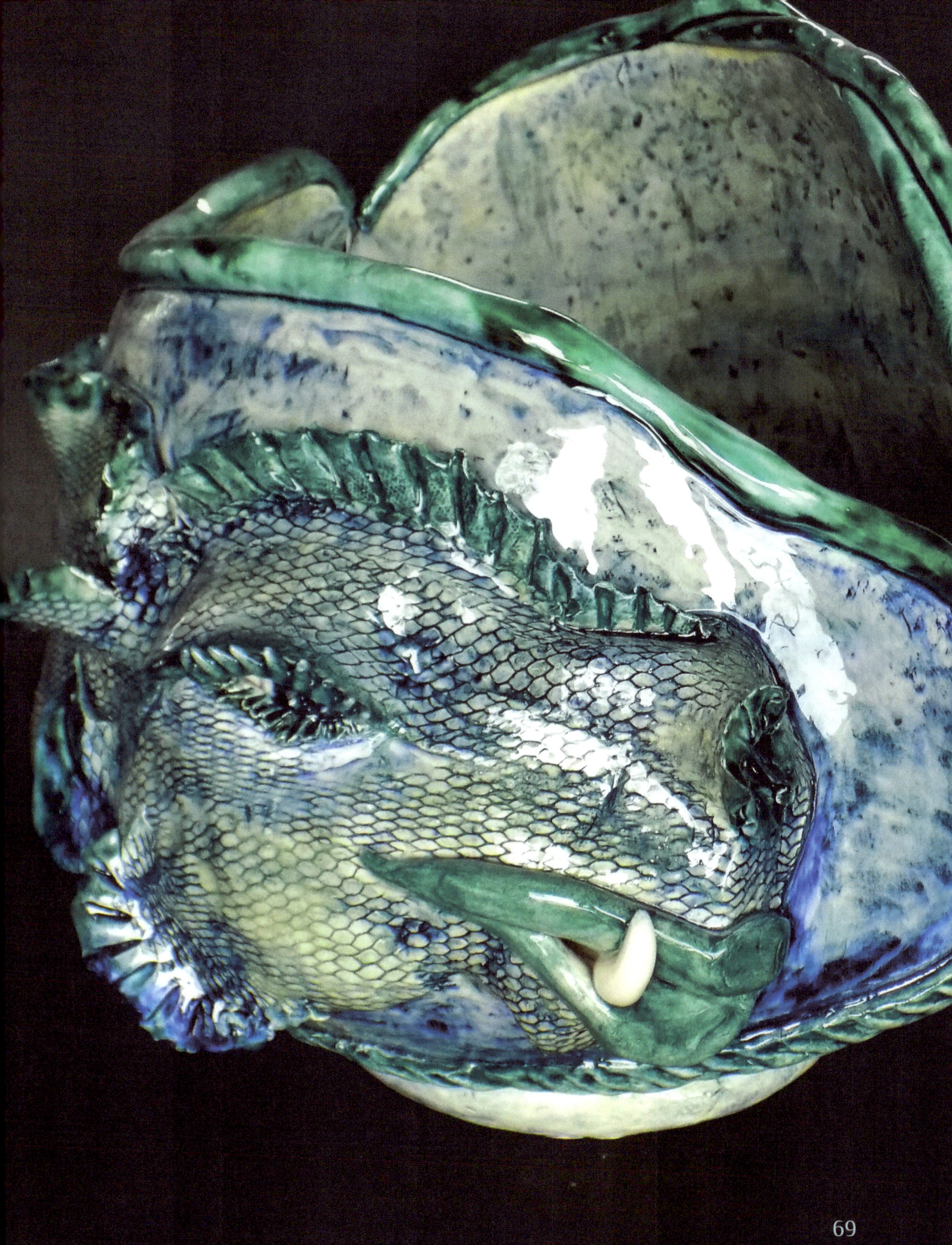

The Sun Dragon floated slowly across the sky, over Dragon Island. Everywhere he looked, he saw someone preparing for the big celebration. The Day Dragon had been gone for several days, busy inviting every dragon she could find. The larder was filling up. The Sun Dragon had seen to most of it himself. The Night Dragon and Young River had to temporarily cease their lessons, in order to prepare the island for all the guests. The Ice Dragon arrived with a much smaller iceberg in tow. Without the help of The Sea Dragon, it was all she could manage. Sun called down to her from above, "Hail Ice, it is a good day to push icebergs." "Hello Sun," said Ice, "Would you mind keeping your distance from my berg? I don't want it to melt before the party even starts!" "Of course, my dear," replied Sun. "May I send you some help?" "Send River out to help transport all this fish into the larder," said Ice. She had ice-blasted several tons of arctic fish into a large, frozen block.

When River arrived, he found that the fish block floated and could be easily pushed ashore. He thought it was the most fun job that he was ever given, until he got the block to the beach. It was so large that he couldn't budge it any further. Night saw his struggle and came over to assist him. "May I help you, River?" River looked up. "I think you'd better, or all this fish is going to thaw all over the beach." Together, they managed to move the ice block the few hundred feet to the larder cave. Several fish had become dislodged in transit. River and Night made a game of seeing who could snap up the greatest number of loose fish. Ice arrived as they crunched up the last of the fish. She gave them a long look and ice-blasted the larder entrance to preserve its contents "You don't expect us to do all this labor without food, do you?" asked Night. "Of course not," replied Ice, "It's just that you seem to have become as young as River here. I'm not sure that you are mature enough to mentor him." "I'm older than this planet, if I am not yet mature, I think I never will be!" said Night, with a hearty laugh. "Do not lose sight of the fact that life is to be enjoyed, dear Ice." "You are right, dear Night, why else are we bothering to have a celebration?" said Ice, "Now get back to work you two, or your guests will not enjoy themselves." With that, Ice returned to ready her iceberg. River and Night went to clean up the dancing grounds.

The time of the party quickly arrived. Everyone The Day Dragon invited had agreed to come. There were to be almost as many guests as at the annual gathering, maybe more, if The Sea Dragon showed up with an entourage from the deep ocean. Dragons tend to be solitary creatures, but, as Night pointed out, they all believed life is to be enjoyed, so most would not pass up an invitation to celebrate. Day had told everyone that they were celebrating 'the mentoring of The Young River Dragon, by The Illustrious Night Dragon.' While not everyone understood exactly what that meant, they all revered The Night Dragon as one of the first dragons, and came to honor this effort, whatever it was.

That morning, The Sea Dragon did indeed arrive with a large group from the deep ocean! Sea dragons of all shapes and descriptions, along with a few merpeople, set up a sort of camp in the lagoon. None of them had been to Dragon Island before, so several young dragons were conscripted to act as tour guides for the newcomers. River took Icthianna and four other young sea dragons, who turned out to be more half-siblings, on a tour around the island. He had been coming here as long as he could remember, so he knew every inch of the island and its surrounding waters. River had a great time with his new-found siblings, and was proud to show off his knowledge of the area.

The Night Dragon spotted Icthianna in the distance, with River, and was struck once again by her beauty. 'How is it that her magic is so powerful, even this far away?' he thought. He began to feel slightly off balance, as if he was dizzy, or drunk on Dragon Juice. 'I will never make it through the party like this!' Nothing would stop The Night Dragon from getting to know The Merdragon better by tonight. He decided to nap, before the festivities, so that he would be at his best. He dreamed of Icthianna.

When the sun began to dip low in the sky, and color the horizon with a brilliant display of oranges and pinks, everyone began moving to the dancing grounds. The Ice Dragon called the group to order, and like the naming ceremony, they all formed a giant circle. River, Night, Cloud and Ocean came into the center, with Ice, who said "I make this proclamation before all the dragons present, that The Illustrious Night Dragon has agreed to mentor The Young River Dragon, teaching him in the ways of all dragons, until such time as he begins his formal dragon schooling. His mother, The Beautiful Cloud Dragon, and his father, The Nobel Ocean Dragon, with much concern for Young River's benefit and well-being, have agreed to this situation." Cloud and Ocean stepped forward and bowed to The Ice Dragon. "I commend The Night Dragon for his thoughtful consideration and concern for the proper education of Young River, and I encourage all adult dragons to step up to ensure the proper education of our youth. We dragons are few, in the Universe, but we are given the great charge of long life and great wisdom, above other creatures. We must make sure that our ways and traditions are passed down to all dragons, everywhere. We must forge an unbroken chain of knowledge from our beginnings, into eternity." The Ice Dragon let out a roar that reverberated over the island and out into the sea, which sealed her proclamation for all time. It was a pivotal moment in dragon history!

The gathered circle of dragons let out their own roars, sealing their approval of Ice's proclamation. Night slapped River on the back. "That makes it official, I guess, River. What do you think?" River looked up at Night and said "This is the most fun I've ever had in my life!" All the dragons pressed in, congratulating everyone. Cloud gave Night a hug, then River. Ocean and Night bowed to one another. The Sun Dragon congratulated all parties, then shouted "Let the festivities begin!" The Day Dragon signaled the dancing drums to begin, and a procession of food was brought out of the larder. Songs were sung, food and drink flowed freely, and dancing went on and on.

The Night Dragon found Icthianna hovering off to the side of the displayed edibles, and asked her, "How are you enjoying the party, my dear?" "I've never seen anything like it!" answered Icthianna. "Would you care to dance?" asked Night. "I have never danced in the air before" she said. "It is easy" replied Night, "Just take my hand and follow me." Icthianna said "I'm afraid I swim much better than I fly." "Don't worry, my dear, I will help you" said Night. He lifted her off the ground with one finger, as he rose into the air. She found herself suddenly as weightless as if she were swimming in very salty water, only she was surrounded by warm tropical air. They danced for a long time, until Icthianna said "I don't want to stop dancing, dear Night, but I feel like I am drying up!" "No problem, my dear," said Night, and they drifted to the ground, some distance from the merriment, to a cozy cove.

"Oh, thank you Night" she said, as she dropped into the water. She disappeared for a moment, then popped up by Night's tail. "Can you swim?" she asked. "River has been teaching me, but I seem to need to keep my head above the water, or I start to spew smoke" replied Night. "That's ok, we can keep our heads above the waves" said Icthianna" I can still hear the drums, we can dance here!" Night found that the lagoon was shallow enough that he didn't need to do all that much swimming; he could stand on the bottom and dance with the beautiful Icthianna. He thought that he must be the happiest dragon on the planet.

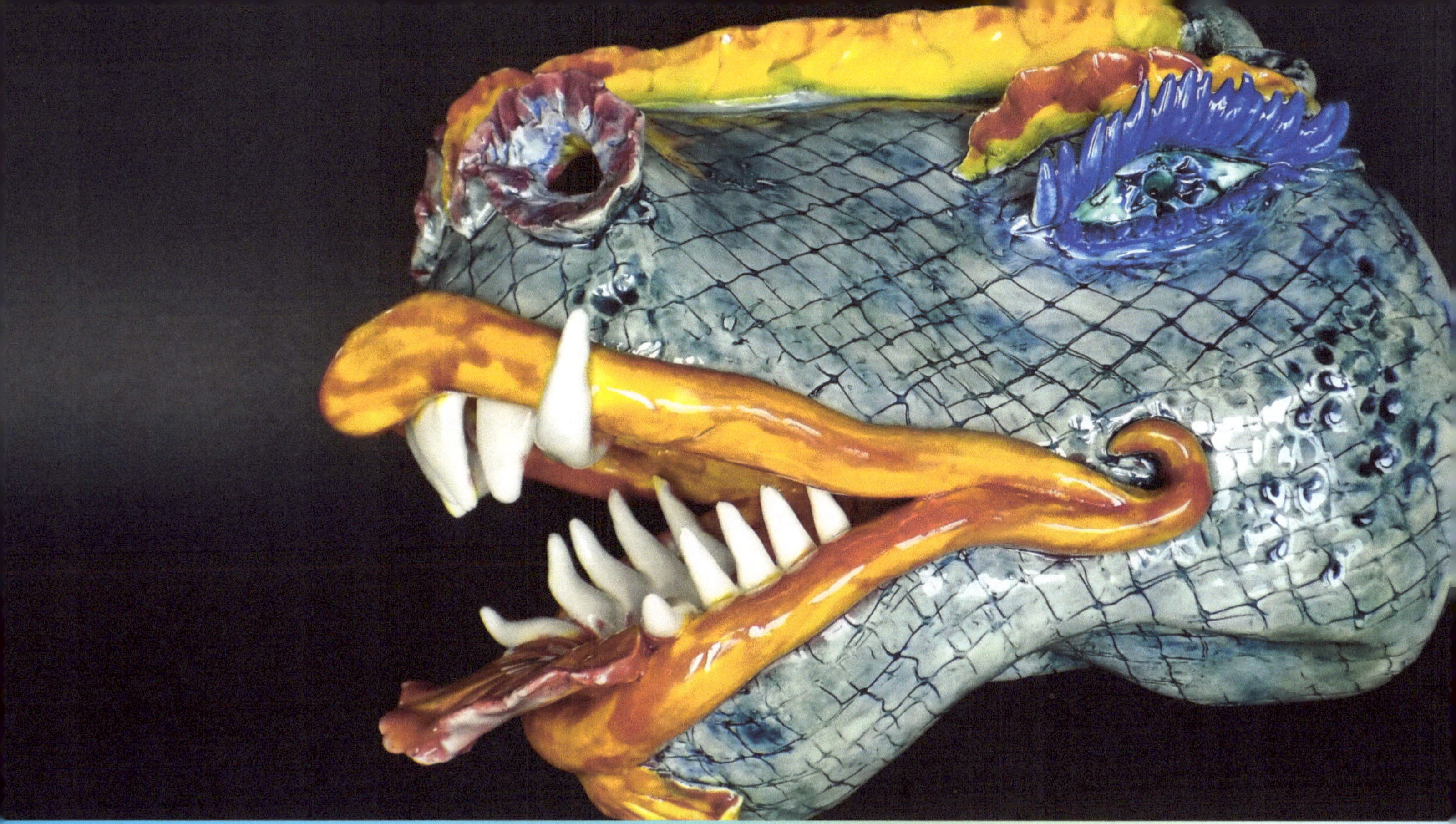

River and Rain had great fun with their new-found siblings. They ate their fill of the delicacies, then went down to the main lagoon to play. When they tired themselves out, they sat on the rocks of the sea platform. "So, how come no one is mentoring you, Rain?" asked a dragon named Coral. "You are in the same situation as River, aren't you?" "Oh, I'm older than River," said Rain. "I'll start my formal schooling in only a few years." "I was wondering that too," said River. "You should join Night and me, he is so much fun!" "I don't know," said Rain. "I'm pretty busy in the rain forest, you know." "I'm going to ask Night if you can join us sometimes," said River. "It will be fun." The group of young dragons fell into telling each other about their lives, laughing and enjoying the comradery of shared youth. They all eventually dozed off, either on the rocks, or beneath the gentle waves.

The Night Dragon and The Merdragon settled themselves on some rocks, he above and she mostly below the water. After a short time of silence, Night asked Icthianna what had been a burning question, in his mind, for some time. "How did such a wondrous creature as yourself, come to be?" "You mean how did a dragon and a mermaid get together?" asked Icthianna. "Well yes, tell me your history, if you would" said Night "As far as you are comfortable in telling me." "Oh, it is a well-known story in my ocean. Better that you hear it from me than someone else." said Icthianna.

"The merpeople have lived with the sea dragons for a long time. Not always peacefully. We compete for food and resources. There was finally peace between mer and dragon, after The Ocean Dragon began to rule. He and my mergrandfather made a kind of treaty, and to seal the peace, Ocean agreed to wed my mother. She is one of my grandfather, The Merking's daughters. Well, dragons don't marry, they mate by mutual agreement, merpeople marry for life. They each stepped out of their traditional roles, for the good of the ocean and to preserve the peace." Night looked on in wrapped silence. She continued "I am the child they created, I am sometimes called 'Peace Incarnate' but I prefer my mermaid name." "Did they use magic to be able to create you?" asked Night.

"Oh, I am definitely a magical creation, I can do things that neither dragon nor mermaid can do. When I am in the mer-kingdom, I am treated as a goddess. The dragons pretty much treat me as myself. I think I prefer spending time with my dragon relatives, there is much less pressure to be... oh I don't have a word for it." She put up her hands. The Night Dragon looked at Icthianna and said, "Feel free to just be yourself with me, my dear. We dragons know that we are all gods, each with our own talents and powers. We seldom flaunt our differences, we honor our own individual talents." "Yes, that's it exactly!" said Icthianna. "The dragons like me for me, not for my talents. You are so wise, Night." "My wisdom comes from being around since the planet was made, merpeople are just newcomers by my timeline, though they probably don't see it that way," said Night. "Do you spend much time with your mer-family?" "I spent my first thousand years with my mother and her family. I have been living with my father for about 300 years," said Icthianna. "Many of the young merpeople work for Ocean, so I see my mer-friends and relatives often. I return to sit as a goddess, several times each year, for festivals and such." "It sounds to be a very full life," said Night. "Are you happy?" "I think so," said Icthianna. "Though this is the first time I have ever left my ocean. I think it might seem boring when I go back!" Icthianna shifted on the rocks, so that her head rested on Night's foot. She soon fell asleep. Night thought it was the sweetest thing he had ever felt; he never wanted to move. After a long time of watching Icthianna sleep, he dozed off himself.

Some hours after the sun rose over Dragon Island, everyone began to stir. The remnants of the larder were brought out, and promptly devoured. Dragons began their journeys home. They all seemed happy, if tired. The Sun Dragon circled the Island, thanking the guests for coming and wishing them safe travel home. The Sea Dragon's group gathered in the lagoon, preparing to swim back to their ocean homes.

All the young water dragons were put to work, along with the few merpeople who had come along, tidying up the shore, and rooting out what sea life they could find for their long trip.

Day, River, Rain and Smoke set to work cleaning up the island. Late in the morning, the remaining group met at the dancing grounds. The Sun Dragon landed in the middle of them and said, "Well done, everyone. The party seems to have been a great success." The Day Dragon said "I want to thank each one of you for making our party an event to remember! You made my job of hostess so easy, perhaps we should do this every year, at the solstice." The Sun Dragon said, "Let's not get carried away, my dear. Maybe we could try once every 100 years, and see how that goes." The crowd chuckled, they all knew that the females would find a reason to celebrate something, long before then. With a long look from Day, she and Sun rose into the air and began their trip home.

The Night Dragon watched them fly off together and wondered if they were now a mated pair. He looked down, Icthianna was still at his side. She looked at him and said, "It is time for me to go, dear Night. My father and his group are gathering at the end of the lagoon." "I wish you could stay, dear one, there is so much I would like to share with you," said Night. "I feel the same way," said Icthianna. "Perhaps you and River could visit my ocean soon?" "Certainly, my dear, I would like that very much. It would be good for River to spend time with his relatives, if he doesn't have to swim too deep in the ocean." "He did have a good time with his half-siblings, and they enjoyed him also. I'm sure they would be willing to spend time with him in the mermaid lagoon," said Icthianna. "If the merpeople don't mind," said Night. "Oh, if I am with them there can be no discord, I am Peace Incarnate, after all." "You should speak with The Moon Dragon," said Night. "Her mission in the world is peace." "I would love to," said Icthianna. "Tell her I will watch for her, the next time the full moon passes over my ocean." "I will be sure to inform her, I see her often, when I hunt," replied Night.

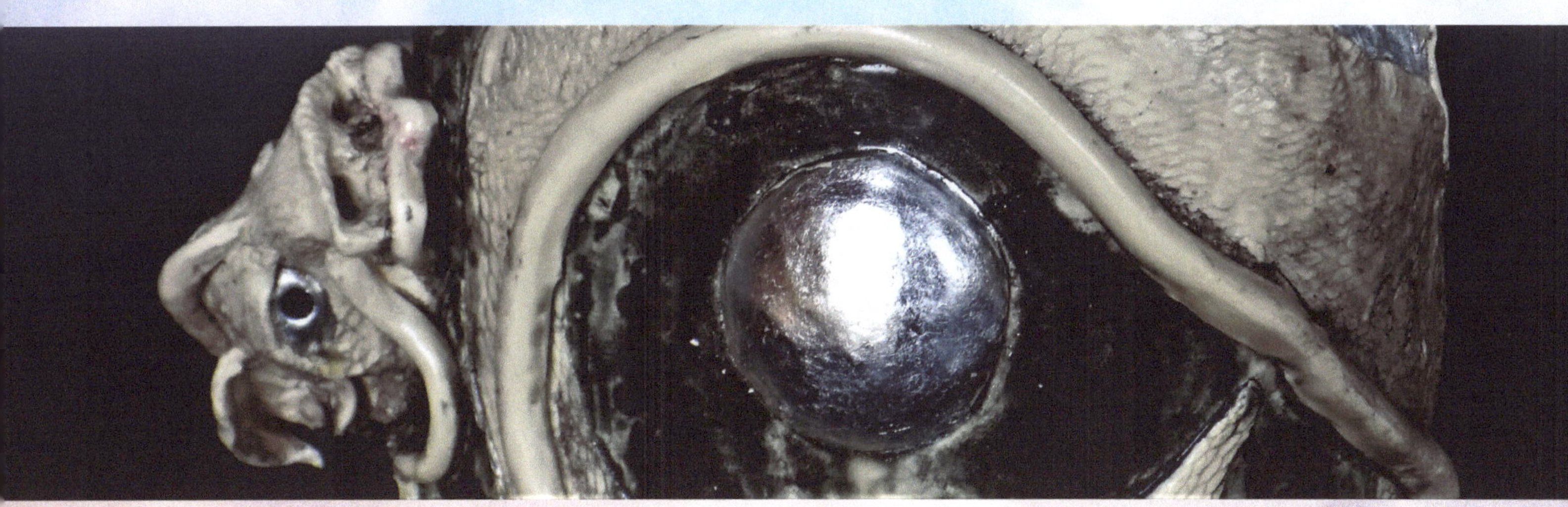

The merpeople in the lagoon began blowing on conch shells. The sound echoed over the water. "That is the signal to leave, I'm afraid," said Icthianna. "Never be afraid dear one, that is the first rule of being a dragon!" said Night. "I promise that we will see each other again soon," said Icthianna, as she flew up and kissed him on the nose. Then she dove into the water, to join her family. Night watched as her tail flipped her down under the waves.

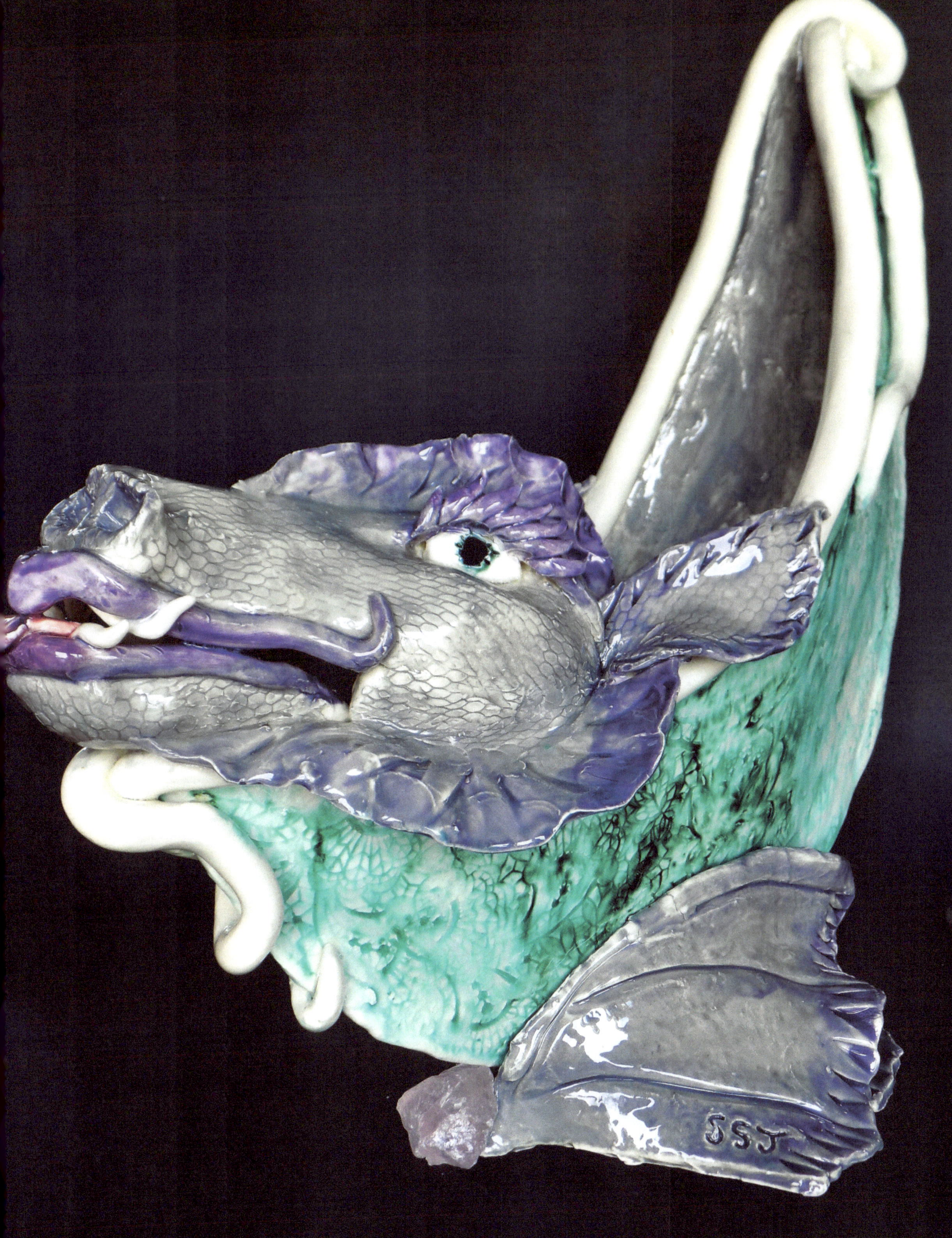

A few weeks later, **Night and River** arrived at the mermaid lagoon. To their surprise and delight, they found lcthianna and The Moon Dragon, in deep discussion, perched on the rocky shore. "Greetings fair ones," said Night, with a bow. "Greetings dear sister and lllustrious Moon Dragon," said River, with his own deep bow. Moon and lcthianna returned the bows of greeting. The Moon Dragon said, "Hail Noble Dragons, how fortunate that you find us this evening." "How so?" asked Night. "lcthianna has come up with an interesting idea, but it may require both of you to help," said Moon. "Anything for dear lcthianna," said Night. "Anything for my sister," said River.

And so, it was that Icthianna and The Night Dragon came to open a school for young dragons. They began in the mermaid lagoon, but soon moved to an island, several miles offshore. Here they tutor both sea and land dragons. Night even built a library, to house his collection of books. All the adult dragons come to take turns giving lessons to the young. They each come for a month's stay and teach whatever skills they feel they know best. Even The Ocean Dragon approves, because he supplies the school with food from his ocean farming operation, giving ample work to all merpeople and sea dragons.

The young dragons turned out to love all the camaraderie and classes that the school provides.

Icthianna loves overseeing the school, she also loves The Night Dragon. Night spends most of his time at the school, so he can be near Icthianna. They've grown as close as two beings can be.

River is perhaps the happiest of all, because he has something new and interesting to do every day.

ABOUT THE AUTHOR

Susan Smith James is an artist, who lives on a farm in southern New Jersey. She spent many years as a full-time potter. She found that the responsibilities of raising her two sons and caring for the farm, with her husband, took up all her time. Working in clay became more of a wish than an actuality. When her youngest son went off to college, she found that dragons were tapping on her shoulder, asking her to construct pots of them. After she had made several dragon pots, they began sharing their conversations with her, and the beginnings of this book took shape.

www.DancingDragonMagic.com